Owned Men II

*A Collection of Fetishistic
Short Stories*

Owned Men II

*A Collection of Fetishistic
Short Stories*

First Edition

Published by the Nazca Plains Corporation
Las Vegas, Nevada
2017

ISBN: 978-1-61098-399-0
E-Book: 978-1-61098-400-3
Published by
The Nazca Plains Corporation®

Printed in the United States of America.

PUBLISHER'S NOTE
Owned Men II is a work of fiction created wholly by Christopher Trevor's imagination. All characters are fictional and any resemblance to any persons living or deceased is purely by accident. No portion of this book reflects any real persons or events.

Proofreader, Joseph Measel
Art Director, Joseph Measel
Cover Photography, llhedgehogll

**In loving Memory of Stanley,
A.K.A. Hryhoots,**

who always believed in my work...

Owned Men II

by Christopher Trevor

Acknowledgements

At this point in time I'm a fifty-something year old writer who is as thankful to be published with book number thirty-something as he was when he was published with his first two books.

For the last thirteen years, I have helped men's feet fetish, man-to-man tickling, man-to-man bondage and even male and female erotica become more mainstream and understood. *Understood*... did I really just say that? Because most of the time I myself don't understand the material I write about. But nonetheless writing it all and continuing to write it and seeing it published has brought me happiness and elation that I cannot fully describe.

There is definitely something about a handsome man in black socks that appeals to so many of us. Regardless of how that man is interpreted in my fiction, from perhaps Timmy Backman being captured yet again and relentlessly tickle tortured, on his black socked feet to perhaps my erotic muse, John Robinson, bound up tight once again by Captor and struggling to get himself free, clad in just his black dress socks of course.

Timmy Backman, Cleeve and Otis, and John Robinson, I thank them all, as they are the best known, most enduring of all the characters I have brought to life thus far. Of course, I should also mention and thank Ronald Greene, Valerie Levi and Makya Leekalot, seeing as without them Timmy Backman would never wind up in the tickle trouble he always finds himself in.

I have humbly accepted my role in causing men who never gave a thought to their black dress socks as they get dressed for work in the morning to somehow become aroused now when they put those socks on before climbing into their business suit. I've had guys, both gay and straight, and I thank them all, tell me that until they read my work they had never thought of their black dress socks as erotic in any way.

I am always surprised and amazed that so many men have chosen to share this newfound secret of theirs with me. Because you see, it simply fans the fires for more stories to be born in my ever-twisted creative imagination.

What I also love about writing this sort of erotica is the mystery that surrounds it, the mystery that will NEVER be solved. The mystery being, what is it about a guy wearing black socks that so drives so many of us wild with lust? What is it about that guy in his black socks that so fuels my imagination and causes the sort of stories I write to be born?

When I am asked these questions by readers and even non-readers of my work I'm never really able to offer a plausible answer. I simply say, "It's a mystery to me and I love it that way."

So please, as you now sit there with my latest book in hand, please enjoy more of my mysteries... Happy Reading and thank you again for your interest in my work...

– Christopher Trevor

Contents

Introduction

by Linda Eden

"You guys want to what?" is how the book begins, where a handsome napping, on vacation at his sister's house, Wall Street executive is awakened by his nephew and a buddy of his nephew's. We never hear the question that was posed to the napper, a guy named Scott, as he lay stretched out on the couch, but for the reader's benefit he repeats the question asked by either his nephew, or his nephew's buddy, we never know which. And it is this question that sets us off, us readers, on Christopher Trevor's latest collection of erotic and in some sections, sinister short stories, this time aptly titled, "Owned Men II."

The second story, "Mark Jostad Tells his Lunch Hour Story is yet another exploration of Mr. Trevor's of the perils that can befall an unwitting executive during something as usual and everyday as lunch hour. Obviously this story is a sort of flashback to "Lunch Hour", which appeared in Christopher Trevor's second book, "Executive Ties that Bind", the difference here though being that the lunch hour victim reveals to his buddies what befell him, while in the first "Lunch Hour" the victimized executive was too humiliated to reveal what had happened to him... AND, like in the first Lunch Hour we're also treated to another jaw dropping Christopher Trevor story conclusion.

Besides being a fetishist for men's feet and all things connected to them the author is also a true fetishist when it comes to male-to-male discipline. This particular fetish is visited here yet again in the aptly titled "Mr. Flogger."

"I had originally planned to use my recurring character of Master Jeff as the college dean who metes out the discipline in this story." Mr. Trevor has said. "But Master Jeff is not a college dean and he spanks, he does not flog. So I figured a new character was called for here."

As time has gone on Christopher Trevor has stated that since he was a young child he has suffered from clinical depression and irrational fears and phobias. Many of these phobias have been eroticized in many of the author's past thirty plus books. But in the story "Family Picnic Gone Awry", the author says he has now explored a fear that he has had since he was a child, that fear being of his father being kidnapped and him never seeing his father again.

"It can be said I've had Daddy issues all my life," Christopher states. "Given that for a good part of my younger years I mostly feared my father, and then as I grew older, because of personal circumstances, I and my father became very close. One can understand where my mixed feelings come from. For whatever the reason I always feared my father being taken from me... and now, in a way he has been taken from me, in the form of Alzheimer's disease. But to deal with my Daddy issues in a more positive and humorous fashion I wrote "the story "Family Picnic Gone Awry." And yes, there will be more Daddy issues stories down the line."

Down the line, or perhaps right here in this book right now Mr. Trevor? With the story "Dad's Feet", we are treated to yet another handsome napper, but unlike in the opening story in this book, "You Guys Want to What?" this time it's a buddies dad who falls victim to a couple of fetishist's wiles.

And where the never-sending spiral of fetishes that Mr. Trevor writes about are concerned we are offered yet another of the author's recurring fascinations, that being a fetish and outright lust for the military, men in uniforms and a man being repeatedly forced to ejaculate. The sleazy and mysterious bar, "The Local" is once again the setting for an unwitting victim of the infamous and torturous glory hole, this time a ruggedly handsome soldier named "Soldier boy McCann."

A Christopher Trevor collection of short stories would hardly be complete without a male tickle torture tale somewhere in the mix. For this purpose the author turned to his archives and returned to the beginning, with a story he penned back in the late 1990s, titled, "Tickling Arthur's Feet."

"There was so much inspiration for this story that I would hardly know where to begin," says Mr. Trevor. "Let's just say that the inspiration came mostly from a handsome suit I used to see on the train many, many years ago at this point, an asshole I worked with at my first full-time job, a now defunct website called Ropejock.com and a sudden urge to write a LONG tickle torture tale."

The book is rounded out with three, what the author calls, "Bonus (boner?) tales." In the story "Ethan's Feet", the author explores yet another fetish where men's feet are concerned. In this case it is sandaled and bare feet. In "Benny Addiction", a strange doctor and patient relationship is explored and lastly, "Car Ride" marks the return of Christopher Trevor's buddy, Ron Bossman.

Happy Reading

-Linda Eden

You Guys Want to What?

"You guys want to what?" Scott exclaimed, not believing what he had just heard his nephew Alex say, as the young twenty year old blond lanky guy stood next to his best buddy, a guy named Caleb, he with dark hair and dark sinister looking eyes… and from the tight tee shirt he was wearing it was obvious that Caleb had muscles to spare. "Did you just say you wanted *to lick* my goddamned feet? Is that what you said? Seriously? You asked to lick my feet? With my socks on them no less at that? *Lick my feet?*"

"Come on Uncle Scott, you'll love it, *and* you have *great* looking socked feet, especially in those thin Gold Toe nylon numbers you're wearing at the moment," Alex chuckled as he and Caleb stood next to the bed in the guest room where his uncle was staying while a guest at his parent's house, Scott being Alex's mother's brother. "Feet like yours are *meant* to be worshipped in that way, to have a couple of dudes lick 'em for you, really lick and even suck your toes through that gold toe material. *That* will really make you feel great."

Looking up Scott said, "I don't believe what I'm hearing here, *I do not believe this Alex.* Never before in all my life… holy shit… You and your buddy there want to lick my feet? Lick my goddamned smelly feet while I have my socks on, what you just called my Gold Toe nylon numbers? Of all things? *Of all fucking things Alex?"*

"Sure thing Uncle Scott, since you've been staying here all week all you've done is parade around the house in white sweat socks, not that I'm complaining mind you, your feet look great in white socks as well, but today you look especially awesome in those navy blue nylon dress socks you're wearing," Alex said, sounding totally confident in all that he was suggesting where his uncle's socked feet were concerned, and Scott saw that as Alex was speaking his buddy, Caleb was licking his lips hungrily. "And when I told my buddy Caleb here about you and your socked feet, well, we talked it over and we just figured we would do you the honor of lick worshipping those socked feet of yours. So can we? Please?"

Scott's face took on more of a look of astonishment. Then, he looked down at his navy blue socked feet and wiggled his toes.

"Jeez, yeah, navy blue socks I wore today, didn't even give it a thought when I got dressed this morning, I guess I'm just one of those dudes who doesn't pay much attention to his socks, of all things, my damned socks huh?" Scott said musingly, grinning a bit now. "When I packed my bags for my trip here I just grabbed a bunch of my socks from my sock drawer, didn't even give it a thought that one of those pairs was a pair of my more dressy numbers, huh. And now my nephew and his buddy want to lick my feet in those blue nylon stinkers I got on..."

"Sure thing Scott, Sir," Caleb said, the first words he had spoken since Scott had woken up from a nap and found the two young men standing over him. "And your nephew here *is* very correct and on the mark. You have *great* looking socked feet. Personally, I find your arches to be very shapely and downright sexy, very masculine looking arches you have Sir."

Looking across himself with his head raised up off his pillow Scott said, "Sexy arches, jeez, *I got sexy arches*... and you *probably* want to lick those arches of mine as well, WITH my socks on of course..."

"Yes Sir, lick them till *your* heart's content," Caleb said, the muscles in his huge arms flexing involuntarily it seemed to Scott.

"Damn, a guy simply decides to take an afternoon power nap and when he wakes up his nephew and his nephew's buddy want to lick his socked feet," Scott said, sitting up and smiling from ear to ear, and scratching his head in a gesture of still disbelief.

"Yeah, a power nap in power socks," Caleb said.

"P-power socks?" Scott asked.

"Yes Sir, a man's dress socks are like his suit and tie, his power suit and power tie, so of course the socks he wears with that power suit and power tie *are* his power socks," Caleb explained and the look of astonishment on Scott's face turned to one of outright confusion.

"So, let me understand this here. What you're saying then is that my white sweat socks, my more casual socks *are not* my power socks, even though I wear them when I work out lifting weights like an animal," Scott said bemusedly.

"It's more a psychological power thing Sir," Caleb went on. "Most men who are executives and in positions of high-power in the corporate world wear dress socks, power socks if you would…"

"You guys really got my head spinning here I got to tell you," Scott chuckled, nodding his head from side to side. "I mean, yeah, I wear suits and ties for my Wall Street job in Manhattan, and I *always* wear nice looking dress socks with those suits and ties of mine, but I never, ever thought of my damned socks as power socks… *of all things*… of all the blasted things, I've learned today that my dress socks are my power socks… and how about that huh?"

"Enough talk Uncle Scott," Alex said then, hunkered down at the end of the bed at his uncle's navy blue socked feet, gripped his left foot and pressed his nose and mouth against the bottom of it.

"H-HEY, I never said it was cool to lick my socked feet Alex!" Scott gasped as chills suddenly sped through his being as his nephew was *instantly* licking the bottom of his left foot up and down and up and down at what felt like breakneck speed. "OH holy shit on a shingle but that does feel awesome at that…"

Grinning devilishly, Caleb moved from the side of the bed, hunkered down next to Alex and gripped Scott's right socked foot in both his VERY strong hands. He leaned his head down and pressed his nose and mouth against the gold material around Scott's socked toes. He inhaled deeply the delicious musty aroma and then lapped a few of those socked toes greedily into his mouth… and went to work sucking the fuck out of them…

"AWWW… AWWW *my God* you guys, you fucking guys, fucking fucks," Scott panted, resting up on his elbows now as his nephew and Caleb serviced his socked feet. "If anyone told me that when I came here to visit my sister and her husband for the week that I would wind up having my damned smelly socked feet serviced this way I NEVER would have believed it, DAMN…"

Scott grunted deeply and gasped real throatily as his nephew continued his up and down licking of the bottom of his left foot, sucking at it in between as well AND Caleb sucked a few of his toes as if they were cocks, his head bobbing up and down as he did so…

"FUCCCKKK, never before in all my life, got two dudes worshiping my stinking socked feet," Scott bantered. "None of the women I ever dated went after my feet, fucking fucks and shit on a shingle…"

The two young men held tightly to Scott's feet as they went on and on sucking and licking them…

A few moments later Alex was sucking the toes on his uncle's left foot as Caleb was now licking the bottom of Scott's right foot in an up and down motion.

"Fuck, you guys sure are in synch here I got to say," Scott chuckled.

As Caleb trailed his tongue up and down the bottom of Scott's right foot he moved his big hands under the man's jeans, caressing Scott's socked calves as he did so.

"MMM, they're OTC's these power socks your uncle has on," Caleb said to Alex and then not only licked the bottom of Scott's socked foot, but started planting hard and powerful kisses and smooches on it. "Fucking love over the calf power socks Sir…"

"Real glad to hear that dude," Scott chuckled. "But to tell it truthfully and to the point here the only reason I wear those OTC power socks is so when I'm in a meeting at work and if I cross one leg over the other I don't show any leg skin," Scott explained as more and more chills engulfed him... AND... he even felt his cock beginning to engorge in his jeans.

"Personally I find it to be real sexy when a guy in calf length dress socks crosses his leg and shows off a patch of leg skin," Caleb said.

"OH yeah, and HAR, HAR for me eh?" Scott asked, grinning stupidly at Caleb. "I wouldn't look all that sexy showing off my hairy legs between my sock and pants leg in a business meeting, you're going to have to trust me on that one dude."

Then, a few moments later Alex and Caleb were both holding one of Scott's feet tightly in their hands and they were both licking and sucking his deep sexy arches.

"AWWW, holy fuck and shit on a shingle you dudes, but *that* is amazing, never thought that my arches could be a damned erogenous zone, of all things, of all the blasted things..." Scott exclaimed and the huge bulge now in his jeans was proof positive of the pleasure he was enduring at the mouths of his nephew and his nephew's buddy on his socked feet. "Damn guys, I'm harder than Chinese arithmetic in my jeans here. Jeez, but what you guys are doing to my damned socked feet is REALLY getting me all worked up in my funky place..."

"Yep, very true to form Uncle Scott, most men have no idea just how sexually sensitive their feet can be," Alex said, pressed his mouth hard against his uncle's arch, gripped his socked foot tighter and sucked that arch at what felt to Scott like a vacuum cleaner turned up to full power. "We're pretty worked up the same way, and that's just from what we're doing to your sweet socked feet here."

"OOO, God that is miraculous Alex," Scott panted. "Looks to me like I'm gonna be wearing my power socks more often from here on out, AND have my future dates worship my feet... WITH those power socks on them."

"Sounds like a good deal Sir," Caleb said, grinning up at Scott, holding his foot tight as his buddy's uncle gasped with his handsome head arched back a bit.

"Yeah, and I can't believe that my smelly socks are a turn-on for you guys," Scott laughed.

"The manly scent is all part of the draw Sir," Caleb said and then… he and Alex stopped servicing Scott's socked feet for a moment, held those size elevens in hand, looked at each other and grinned devilishly. "Now Alex?"

"Now Caleb," Alex said.

Caleb let go of Scott's foot that he was presently servicing, moved to the side of the bed, reached down, and as Alex then pressed his uncle's socked feet together and began furiously kissing them all over Caleb pulled down the zipper on Alex's uncle's jeans.

"HOOO, oh holy fucks, shit on a shingle, I-I didn't come here for all *this*," Scott panted crazily now, but not making a move to stop Caleb as the young man proceeded to reach into the fly opening of his jeans, past his white briefs and brought out his erect eight inches or so of thick beefy cock and sweaty hairy kiwi-sized testicles.

"No? Where do you usually go for all this?" Caleb asked, leaned down further and slurped Scott's manhood into his mouth… as Alex continued sucking and kissing his socked feet.

"OOOHHH HAR, HAR for me again huh? Very funny you are dude, AWWW but fuck, never had any dudes do to me what you two are doing to me here today," Scott ranted as he writhed in ecstasy as his feet and cock were wonderfully serviced… "JEEZ, and to think I came here just to visit my sister and her hubby…… what a bonus this all is huh?"

"Yes Uncle Scott, a real boner of a bonus, yes?" Alex asked with a grin and sniffed his uncle's gold toes, as Caleb bobbed his head up and down, sucking heartily on Scott's erection, tugging and caressing his testicles at the same time.

"HUUUHHH… fucking dude is gonna get my nut while my nephew licks and sniffs my socked feet, my power socked feet at that," Scott panted, his head arched back on the pillow. "MY GODDD, I'm gonna cum so much that I can't believe it dudes!"

"Actually I can believe it Uncle Scott, having one's feet worshipped this way CAN REALLY make a dude spurt and spray double the amounts he's used to," Alex chuckled, and then, the young man's uncle was grunting like a marine who hadn't cum in months, as Caleb chugged down his frothy offering.

"AAAWWWHHH, AWWW, my God and shit on a shingle!" Scott swore nodding his head rapidly from side to side as his nephew sucked his socked toes while gripping his feet tight and his nephew's buddy GREEDILY sucked every possible drop of sperm from him. "AWWW fucking dudes got me spermming like a mad man here... feels awesome at that I gotta say..."

When Scott was done shooting his load down Caleb's throat the young man let his buddy's uncle's spent manhood slide from his mouth, licking his lips as he did so, that driving the navy blue socked dude even crazier...

"GOD, just came from having my socked feet licked and worshipped, shit on a shingle but what a day this turned out to be," Scott said breathlessly... and then, he watched with a grin as his nephew and Caleb positioned themselves standing over his socked feet, took their cocks out of the fly opening of their jeans... and began stroking each other's pre cum dripping erections... those erection's slits aimed right at Scott's navy blue socked feet. "HA, looks like my power socks are about to get a good soaking huh dudes?"

"Oh yes Uncle Scott, most definitely a good soaking," Alex panted as he stroked Caleb's gigantic cock, the muscular young man's testicles swinging back and forth as he did so.

It took all but just a few minutes and then Scott was watching beguilingly and with a look of total wonderment on his face as his nephew and Caleb shot globs upon globs of their ball juice all over his socked feet, and yes, as Scott had said, soaking his power socks with their messes.

The two young men roared like animals and it seemed to Scott as if their geysers and torrents of messy sperm would never stop...

But stop it did and the two young men stood there panting in ecstasy, holding each other's cocks tight as the last remnants of their offerings dripped from their wide sex slits.

"Fucking beautiful socked feet, what a way to get off huh buddy?" Caleb said to Alex as he and Alex let go of each other's cocks.

"Fucking A bud," Alex replied.

The two young men grinned at each other, nodded up and down and once more hunkered down at Scott's socked feet, his cum soaked socked feet, to be totally precise... and began licking their cum from them...

"AWWW fuck, now that REALLY feels amazing dudes, being that my nylon socks are all slicked with your messes it makes me feel all the more sensitive in my feet, shit on shingle," Scott panted and without even thinking about grabbed his semi hard cock and began stroking it as the two young men sucked and kissed and massaged and worshipped his power socked feet...

After Scott, Alex and Caleb had all shot a second load each Scott watched with a look of glee on his face as his nephew and his buddy walked out of his room, each of them carrying one of his socks with them as a souvenir of their wondrous encounter...

"Fucking shit on a shingle, never before in all my life," Scott laughed and flopped back down on the bed, wiggling his now bare toes with his spent cock still sticking out of the fly opening in his jeans...

Scott lay there for a few minutes, just thinking about all that had just happened and his cock tingled, all slimy with the leftovers of the second load he had just shot...

But then, as he continued to lay there in a state of bliss he heard a gentle knuckle knock on his guest room door, the door that his nephew and his buddy had left open...

"HUH? Oh shit, shit on a shingle," Scott exclaimed in a near panic when he looked up and saw his sister's husband, Dale, standing there, in his suit and tie.

"Hey Scott, how's it uh, how's it going bud? I just uh, just got in from work and wanted to say a quick hello," Dale, a handsome forty something year old banking executive with receding brown hair and brown eyes said as he stepped into Scott's room, gently closing the door behind him.

"UH, yeah, yeah, it's uh, it's going good Dale, was just relaxing you know," Scott hemmed and reached to pack his cock and balls back into the fly opening of his jeans. "And I uh, I can explain this... it's not what you think..."

"Relax bud," Dale said, looking hungrily at Scott's bare feet.

"What are, what are you doing Dale?" Scott asked as Dale hunkered down at the end of the bed, grabbed Scott's naked feet in his hands... and began licking and massaging them, sucking his toes and deep kissing his arches.

Scott's eyes opened wide in astonishment, he said to himself, "Like father like son," grabbed his cock and slowly stroked himself as his brother-in-law now took a turn at his feet... this time with no socks on them...

The End

Mark Jostad tells his Lunch Hour Story

"I don't know if I should be telling you guys about this, but after what happened yesterday in the storage room on the fourth floor I feel like *I have to* tell somebody," Mark Jostad said to his two office buddies, Jim Kelly and Michael Garrett as they sat in the company dining hall having lunch on that Thursday afternoon. "Because I have to say, I still can't believe it happened."

"Can't believe what happened bud?" Jim, a blond haired, blue-eyed fairly muscular guy in a suit and tie asked after swallowing a mouthful of salad.

"Well, you guys know how on every Monday and Wednesday I go down to the fourth floor where that storage room is, where we store our deliveries of office supplies and other crap we purchase?" Mark asked.

"Yeah, sure, you go down there on Mondays and Wednesdays to take an hour long power nap instead of eating lunch," Michael, he with brown hair and green eyes and thin in his suit and tie said. "What's the big deal? Did you get in trouble for sleeping on the job? If that's the case fuck them, it's *your* lunch hour after all."

"No, no, nothing like that bud," Mark said. "Okay, if you two promise to keep this just between us I'll tell you."

"Sure, go ahead, tell us," Jim said. "You've sure got my curiosity piqued off the Richter scale."

Mark put his fork down, took a hearty chug of his Diet Coke and leaned back in his chair, tugging his tie a few times before beginning.

"Okay, so yesterday, like any other Wednesday, at precisely one PM I shucked off my suit jacket, hung it on the back of my desk chair, loosened the knot in my tie, undid the first two buttons of my dress shirt and with a rolled up bath sized towel to rest my head on and my sleep mask in my suit trousers pocket I took the elevator to the fourth floor storage room," Mark began. "I like that storage room because even though stuff is stored in there it's kept really clean. I mean, the cleaning staff even vacuums the rug in there on a daily basis. It's treated as if it were an office, hence the reason I take my twice a week power naps in there. Plus the fourth floor is deserted, so there's no chance of anyone disturbing me while I take my refreshing power nap."

"Yeah, clean as a whistle that room is, with Vice President Stanley Bradshaw and his assistant Marybeth Lopez at the helm of this place everything is kept clean to the point of nearly military codes," Michael chuckled. "But I have to say, in the end it's worth it."

"Yeah, so even an executive like me can stretch out on a rugged floor in a storage room with his shoes off and take a power nap right?" Mark asked.

"Yeah, right, no harm no fouls," Michael said.

"*Wrong*, because yesterday the darndest *damnedest* thing happened to me, or should I say the darndest *damnedest* thing happened to my feet, my goddamned *socked* feet at that," Mark said, angrily forked a mouthful of salad into his craw, chewed and swallowed.

Jim and Michael looked at each other quizzically and then back at their office buddy.

"Y-your socked feet?" Jim asked. "What in all hell are you talking about bud?"

Mark nodded affirmatively and said, "Let me tell it as it happened okay?"

"Sure thing man," Jim said. "Never heard a dude talk about his socked feet though, of all things."

"Yeah, I feel the same way man, I really do, I mean, when do any of us dudes EVER talk about our socks of all things?" Mark said, ate more salad and then went on relating his tale. "Anyway, I get down to the fourth floor storage room, I step inside, place my rolled up bath towel on the floor and sit down on the floor to get my shoes off and my sleep mask on, all ordinary things for a guy to do before he takes his power nap, right?"

Jim and Michael nodded and Mark continued...

"Okay, so there I am, laying stretched out on my back on the rugged floor, totally relaxed, my hands crossed over my chest," Mark went on. "I started doing my deep breathing exercises to really relax myself even further and it was while I was doing that and wiggling my toes, which is also good for the relaxation, when IT happened."

"IT?" Jim asked. "What was IT?"

"They must have already been in the storage room because I hadn't heard the door open after I had settled myself in there," Mark said. "They probably knew that I would be there for my power nap so they waited for me."

"They?" Michael asked. "Who are they?"

"Well, seeing as I had my sleep mask over my eyes that's the million dollar question, the question that I will *never* be able to answer bud," Mark said, sounding angry now. "But I do know that there were two of them... and oh man, did those two, whoever the fuck they were LOVE my damned socked feet."

"Again with your damned socked feet bud?" Jim asked. "We all wear socks; it's a natural guy thing. What all is this about your socked feet while you were power napping?"

"I'm getting to that now," Mark said. "But you won't believe it. I STILL don't believe it!"

Mark's two buddies looked at him expectantly.

"So I'm lying there, totally relaxed, when all of a sudden, from out of nowhere it seemed I felt two strong, two VERY strong hands grab my forearms," Mark explained. "Before I could even try to get my bearings or try to react whoever had me by the forearms pulled my arms from over my chest and to my sides... and then, oh God, and then I heard duct tape being sheared off a roll, no doubt the duct tape having been stored in the storage room... AND THEN, the next thing I knew I was being duct taped to the floor. Fuck, I knew it was two of them because of the way I was being held down by one of them and the other was stretching length after length after length of duct tape over my chest and pressing the ends HARD to the rugged floor. I struggled like a madman, swearing and cursing like a captured marine, demanding to know what kind of foolishness they were heaping on me. But of course I didn't receive any sort of a reply as they went on and on duct taping me to the floor, pinning me there. And fuck, but duct tape is strong buds, and they were shearing it at what seemed like thousands of miles per hour and layering me in it. Once they were done I could not move my upper body to save my life."

"Why would someone do that?" Michael asked.

"Fucking wish I knew," Mark replied. "But it's what happened next that REALLY sent my sleep-masked head spinning. As I was struggling under the layers of duct tape that they had pressed over my upper torso, and as I was cursing and swearing at them I felt a pair of hands grab my feet, *my black socked feet* at that."

"Why the need to describe your socks to the max?" Jim asked. "Black socks are universal. We all wear 'em at one time or another, especially suit guys like us."

"True that," Mark said. "But let me ask you guys this. Have you ever had two dudes go crazy licking your feet, WHILE you were wearing your black socks?"

At the sound of that question both Jim and Michael set their forks down and looked at their buddy with blank expressions on their faces.

"Lick, *lick your feet?*" Michael asked, sounding totally perplexed. "They, whoever "THEY" were, *they licked* your black socked feet?"

Mark nodded affirmatively.

"BUT, but dude, if you're like other dress socked guys out there, and like us, your feet stink in your nylon numbers," Jim said. "Holy fuck... they actually licked your black socked feet while they had you duct taped to the floor in the storage room?"

"That they did, and more," Mark said.

"Damn," Michael said with a grin. "They licked your smelly black socked feet. Let me tell you guys, when I get home at the end of the day, my wife makes me put my socks right into the washing machine. She won't even handle them to put them in the wash, that's how bad they stink after I've worn them all day and had them encased in my leather shoes."

"They seemed to love the stink of my socks," Mark said dejectedly.

"You said they did more than just lick your socked feet bud," Jim said, sounding now like he REALLY wanted to hear Mark's tale.

"Yeah, they not only licked my goddamned socked feet, they sucked my toes through my socks as well, what a thing to happen to a guy huh?" Mark said.

"Holy shit, they sucked your toes too?" Jim asked, sounding astonished.

"Yeah, and you asked bud, so I told you," Mark said sarcastically.

Michael looked down under the table at his feet, his wing-tipped and navy blue socked feet, and said, "Damn, never had any kinky foot action done to these hooves of mine," and laughed.

"So glad you think its funny bud," Mark said sarcastically. "But good as it felt I have to admit I was scared shit-less at the same time."

"It felt good?" Jim asked. "You mean, a married dude like you, it felt good to you to have two guys, TWO GUYS, lick your socked feet?"

"Well fuck buds, let's face it, our feet can be an erogenous zone, studies have proved it, and I was sleep-masked, couldn't see shit, so it could have been *anyone* at my feet," Mark said. "And somehow, the fact that I was wearing thin nylon socks made it feel all the more erotic, even though I was scared shit-less."

"Fuck," Jim whispered.

"So once they had me all taped down to the floor good and fucking tight I felt each of them take one of my feet in their hands, they must have been kneeling on the floor in front of me," Mark went on. "They hoisted my damned socked feet up, cradling them it felt like... and my suit trousers rode down to my knees, really putting my tall socks on display."

"Tall socks?" Michael asked. "What do you mean by that?"

"OTC socks bud, over the calf if you would, socks that come up to just below our knees, socks nice and tall so that if we cross our leg during a meeting we don't risk showing off any leg skin," Mark explained. "Can't believe that two fellow executives like you never knew these things."

"Bud, my wife buys me all my socks and underwear, so really, I just wear whatever the hell is in my sock drawer, you know?" Michael chuckled. "But thanks for the socks education all the same."

"Yeah, you're welcome bud," Mark said cynically. "So anyway there I am, totally helpless, duct taped to the floor, fucking duct taped to the damned floor, sleep-masked, blindfolded as it was... and I feel two dudes lifting my feet and suddenly they're massaging them, running their hands up and down my visible calves.

AND, fuck of fucks I feel them even kissing them, *kissing* my damned calves, sucking on them, holding them tight and aloft. I bobbed my head up and down on my rolled up towel, my teeth were clenched and I was seething at the injustice and depravity of this. I demanded as loudly as I could that they release me and to be quick about it. But instead they held my feet tighter and then I felt their mangy tongues slithering along the tops of them, and I heard them taking deep hearty sniffs of my socked feet as well. After a good fifteen minutes or so of that, from my best estimates mind you, they stopped licking and sniffing the tops of my feet and then grasped them just by the toes. Fuckers squeezed, massaged and kneaded my toes like crazy. And as embarrassed as I am to say it buds, I was hard as a fucking rock in my suit trousers. Can you tell me what was up with that shit? *Seriously, what was it about having two dudes duct tape me to the floor of a storage room and lick my feet and kiss my socked calves that had me so hard in the area of my cock? Can you tell me that?"*

"Well, you yourself said that our feet can be erogenous zones, right?" Jim asked.

"Yeah, I said that huh?" Mark asked.

"Then, they released their grip on my socked toes, moved their hands down to hold my feet then by the arches and center of them... and that's when they sucked my toes, God almighty, they sucked my rancid and stinking socked toes, through my black socks at that," Mark said. But as they sucked my toes I have to say it drove me ape shit, the feelings were electric as they coursed through me."

Michael and Jim looked at Mark intently, all of them seeming to have forgotten their lunch on the table.

"I know, it sounds crazy but it happened buds," Mark went on. They even drooled on my feet and sucked it up. I could feel the warmth of their saliva through my thin socks."

"Fuck, what a thing," Jim said.

"The next thing I knew it felt like they had shifted position and were kneeling on the floor facing me because they were now holding my feet raised... and they were licking the bottoms of them, kissing my socked heels too..." Mark said next.

"Were you still cursing at them bud?" Michael asked.

"What do you think?" Mark asked in response. "Much as I was hard as a damned rock in my suit trousers the last thing I wanted was two dudes licking my damned socked feet, fuck... but remember, even yelling for help would have been fruitless, as that fourth floor where the storage room is, is mostly deserted. The only people who work down there are on the other side of the floor from where the storage room is."

"What a way to spend a lunch hour," Jim chuckled and Mark looked at him angrily. "Sorry bud..."

"Anyway, that was it, my lunch hour, and when lunch hour was over they did the nastiest of possible nasties..." Mark said.

"And what was that?" Michael asked.

"*They*, they unzipped my suit trousers, took my hard cock out of them, along with my balls and started taking turns sucking my cock and licking my balls too," Mark said, looking down at the table as he said it. "And fuck me hard buds, much as I was swearing and cussing at them to stop it, to leave my cock and balls alone, much as I wanted to be released, BUT... but it felt so fucking good, I have to admit it... and when I shot my load they each swallowed some of it, taking turns siphoning it from me it felt like. And I swear, I came like gangbusters, just from having had my socked feet licked and my toes sucked on, go figure huh buds?"

"Yeah, sounds like your feet are most definitely erogenous zones bud," Jim said.

"Your black socked feet at that," Michael said.

"As they sucked my balls dry I called them every word you could think of, perverts, degenerates, rapists... fuckers," Mark said. "But the proof was in the pudding, and in my cum too... what they had done to my socked feet had somehow driven me bonkers."

"How'd you get out of the storage room bud?" Michael asked. "Or did they leave you there when they were done?"

"After they sucked every possible drop of my glop from me they de-socked me, they took my fucking socks, my socks that were now stinking not only of my foot stink but of their saliva as well," Mark said. "I'm guessing they each kept one of my smelly socks as a souvenir of their twisted conquest of me. As for how I got out of the storage room, they loosened the duct tape that was all over me but not enough for me to get free at the moment. They loosened it just enough so they could make their escape before I could get free and take the sleep mask from over my eyes... DAMN..."

"Thank God they didn't hurt you bud," Michael said.

"Nah, I don't think it was ever their intention to hurt me, I think it was more they were some kind of male feet and socks fetishists," Mark said, took a last forkful of his salad, chewed it, swallowed it and looked at his two office buddies.

"It took me a few minutes to get loose from the duct tape and even longer to peel it off my shirt and tie after I pushed my sleep mask up and away from over my eyes," Mark said. "Once I was able to see again I quickly stood up and looked around the room but there was no one there, as if they had never been there. I dashed to the door of the room on my still bare feet, opened the door a bit and looked up and down the hallway, but there was no one there either. They were gone. So with that I put my shoes back on, with no socks no less, collected my towel, took my sleep mask off my head and returned to my office to finish out the day."

Mark looked expectantly at Michael and Jim.

"So, what do you think I should do? Should I report it to Human Resources and Security?" Mark asked.

"I'm not sure," Jim said.

"Yeah, I would bet any amount of money that HR and Security would never have heard anything like that reported before," Michael added. "And you didn't see either of them, so really, what can you report?"

Mark used a cloth napkin to wipe his lips, threw it down on the table and pushed his chair out.

"Yeah, my thoughts exactly," he said as he stood up, took his suit jacket from the back of his chair, pulled it on and looked down at his two still seated buddies. "You two will keep this between us, right?"

"Of course man," Jim said. "No one would believe it anyway."

"But you two believe me right?" Mark asked.

"Of course we do bud," Michael said. "And if you need to ever talk about it again just let us know and we will of course listen again..."

"Thanks guys, see you later," Mark said and walked away from the table, exited the dining hall and headed back to his office.

As soon as Mark was gone Michael and Jim looked at each other, smiled evilly and reached into their suit jacket pockets.

They each brought out a plastic zip-lock bag that contained one black OTC sock each.

The two men picked up their glasses of ice water, clinked their glasses together, sipped and quickly put the bagged socks back into their pockets...

The End

Mr. Flogger

A Discipline Fetish Story

Chapter 1

"Tell me Art, how much money do you think your parents are spending a year to send you here, to this elite, top of the line college so you can study to become a doctor?" the dean of Calder Field College asked the handsome muscular jock-like twenty year old student.

"Uh, I'm really not sure of the *exact* amount Mr. Flogger, Sir, but..." Art began as he sat beside the dean's desk, trembling in nervousness, a feeling of disbelief coursing through him that he had been caught... *found out*... nabbed as it were to the fact that he had been cheating on one of his most recent most very imperative exams.

And to think that the instructor who had turned him in to the dean was the very one he had been giving head to on a regular basis, insuring the fact that he would pass *his* class, no matter what... and now the guy had turned Benedict Arnold on him, Judas as it were and it betrayed the tar out of him...

And now here he was, in the office of the strictest most no nonsense dean at Calder Field College, Mr. Flogger himself... The stories that Arthur Riley, Art to his buddies, had heard where Mr. Flogger was concerned were not pretty. The med student had heard the tales of promising doctors being thrown out of the college on their ear by Mr. Flogger, and for lesser offenses than he had been caught at. He had heard the stories of those up and coming doctors who were now working as file clerks or at other low paying positions in horrible companies... all their dreams up in smoke.

Art knew that he had to find a way to convince Mr. Flogger not to throw him out of the college; his whole future depended on it, not to mention his parent's money that would have been totally wasted on his education at the prestigious institution... DAMN...

And somehow Art Riley knew that Mr. Flogger would not accept a blowjob as payment for turning and looking the other way. Judging from how very hot, ruggedly handsome and well-built the dean was, he could get a blowjob any time he wanted...

Fuck, Art knew he was in really deep shit here...

"Well, seeing as you don't know the exact amount your parents are spending on your education here at Calder Field College let me show you," the dean said and placed a folder in front of the handsome young medical student.

With his fingers trembling Art opened the folder and saw copies of the invoices and checks that his parents had made payable to the college... just so HE would have a proper and elite education. With his fingers still trembling Art held the papers and checks in hand, a feeling of shame and utter disgrace filling him, mostly shame and disgrace at having been caught cheating. His arrogance, even to himself was off the Richter scale.

"So, what do you have to say for yourself Art?" Mr. Flogger asked.

"Nothing Sir, nothing Mr. Flogger, except that I'm sorry, *I'm really sorry*, I don't know what I was thinking," Art said, placing the papers back in the folder and closing it. "And I'm also hoping you won't throw me out of Calder Field. I really want to be a doctor and..."

"Well, usually I would do just that Art, but I've looked over your grades over the last two semesters here at the college, and I know you worked hard for those high grades, I know you didn't cheat to achieve them," Mr. Flogger said. "So you can imagine how surprised I was when Mr. Goldberg brought this cheating incident of yours to my attention."

"Yeah, Mr. Goldberg," Art said distastefully, thinking of the times he had sucked the man's cock in order to earn a good grade.

"So why did you do it Art? Why did you cheat on that test?" Mr. Flogger asked, leaning back in his chair and propping his big size twelve black lace-up well-shined shoed feet on his desk. "Was it maybe you were high on Pot or some other drugs? Maybe that's why you didn't know what you were thinking..."

"NO, no Mr. Flogger, no Sir," Art replied, his lips quivering now, a trembling sound in his voice as he spoke. "I don't do drugs of any sort. I would never..."

Smiling almost devilishly the dean crossed his ankles atop his desk and steepled his fingers over his chest.

"Tell me Art, do you know *why* they call me Mr. Flogger here at Calder Field College?" the dean asked the nervous as all hell student.

"Uh, because it's your name Sir?" Art asked, feeling dumber than a tree as he responded to the dean's question.

The dean smiled from ear to ear...

"No Art, my name is actually Mr. Henshaw, but because of the tactics I use to instill discipline in students, students such as you, I was coined with the nickname of Mr. Flogger," the dean said.

"Oh," Art said numbly. "I see..."

"No you don't Art, at least not yet you don't see, but you will very soon, *very soon you will see why I've been nicknamed Mr. Flogger,*" the dean said slowly. "Take a look at my shoes up there on my desk Art. Take a good look at them."

Art did as the dean said, and turned his attention to the man's shoed feet propped up on his desk.

"What, what about your shoes Mr. Flogger, Sir?" Art asked, as he looked intently at the man's shoes.

"What can you tell me about them Art?" the dean asked.

"Well, they're really nice looking shoes Sir, they're laced up real nice and they're really polished up to what I would call a high gleam," Art said, leaning his face closer to the dean's shoes on the desk. "And uh, well, your black socks match the shoes perfectly."

"You hit it on the head Art; my shoes are polished to a high gleam. I learned to do that when I was in the marine corp.," the dean explained, lifted his feet from the desk, moved them back to the floor and stood up from behind his desk, moving to the side of the desk and standing now over the fear-filled Art Riley. "Did you know that I was in the marines before I came here to Calder Field College Art?"

"No, no Sir Mr. Flogger, I didn't know that you were a marine," Art said.

"Sergeant Flogger I was called," the dean snickered. "Tell me Art, do you know what a flogger is? Do you know what flogging is?"

Before responding Art gulped down a mouthful of fear, and suddenly realized where all this was going. He may have been a dumb jock to some at the college, but he wasn't all that dumb after all..."

"Uh, yes Sir Mr. Flogger, I know what a flogger is, and I know what flogging is," Art said, sounding more and more intimidated now.

"Good man," Mr. Flogger said, now gesturing to the wall where bookcases were filled from top to bottom with encyclopedias. "Okay, now, before we get to what I plan to do to punish you for cheating on Mr. Goldberg's test I want you to take eight encyclopedias from my bookcase there and pile them up in the center of the room in two piles, four to each pile, right under that hook and chain you see soldered to the ceiling up above."

As Art stood up from his chair he glanced over at the encyclopedias and then up at the hook and chain dangling from the ceiling that Mr. Flogger had just mentioned. Once more the young college student swallowed a gulp, a gulp born of fear and total trepidation.

He turned, faced Mr. Flogger and asked, "Mr. Flogger, Sir, what am I in for here?"

The ex-marine smiled evilly and said, "It's to be an old-fashioned form of punishment and discipline Art. You can either accept it or I'll throw you out of the college on your ass. It's up to you..."

Art licked his lips, turned away from the dean and stepped over to the bookcases. He did as he had been told, randomly selected eight of the encyclopedias and made two stacks of them in the center of the room, four to each stack.

"What now Mr. Flogger, Sir... Uh," Art began and when he next looked at the dean his jaw dropped, because the man was holding a black leather flogger in hand.

"Now Art?" the dean asked incredulously. "You're a smart college boy, why don't you tell me what's next?"

"Y-you're going to flog me Sir?" Art asked, tears filling his eyes.

Grinning meanly Mr. Flogger said, "Strip down Art, strip down naked and then prop yourself one foot each on the piles of encyclopedias."

"WHAT?" Art barked then. "You have got to be kidding Mr. Flogger."

"I assure you Art, I'm not kidding," Mr. Flogger stated and swung the lather flogger through the air, it making a bit of a hissing sound, that sound ominous to Art's ears.

"Y-you can't do this, you can't flog a student Mr. Flogger," Art said pleadingly. "Maybe you used to get away with that in the marines, but I assure you... HUUUFFF..."

Art's words were cut short as the dean suddenly delivered a backhanded wallop to his face, sending the handsome college student spiraling backward and landing in a heap on his ass.

"I will only tell you one more time Art, strip down naked and then prop yourself on the encyclopedias," Mr. Flogger said. "If you choose to defy me again you can walk out of here and you will be thrown out of Calder Field College. It's up to you really..."

"I-I'll report you for this," Art tried and the man's grin told him that that would be pointless in the end as well.

"You can do whatever you want Art, but you will still be thrown out of the college for cheating," Mr. Flogger said. "Now, while you strip down I'll lock the door and get the rope that I'll need..."

"Rope?" Art squeaked miserably as he began unbuttoning his shirt.

"Well of course Art, how else am I going to keep you in place?" Mr. Flogger asked and glanced up at the hook dangling from the ceiling.

"Oh my fucks," Art whispered and felt his cock engorging in fear in his pants.

Chapter 2

A short while later, Art Riley found himself positioned atop the two piles of encyclopedias, naked as the day he was born... and holding Mr. Flogger's flogger for the man, while he now stripped down for the chore to come that he would administer to the wayward college boy... but it was the way that Art had been made to hold the flogger that was shocking to the young man, holding it between his teeth, holding it in that fashion because of the way the dean had tied his wrists to a bar above him, a bar that was secured to the dangling hook in the ceiling...

"Feeling good up there Art?" the dean asked the college student as he stood next to him, unbuttoning his shirt now.

"RRRHHH, rho SHIR, rhot rheeling rood rat rall, reeling rared," Art replied, trying to say, "No Sir, not feeling good at all, feeling scared."

Mr. Flogger chuckled as he slowly bared his muscular robust chest, inwardly loving how the bound up stripped Art Riley was watching, watching intently. It always amazed him, even back when he was in the marines how these young men secretly craved these treatments when they had fucked up... how it made their cocks hard to be in the clutches of someone like himself... someone who would show them the error of their ways... and oh they would come back for more... to stay in line as it was...

"Mishter Frogger, rease ron't rog nee, I ronise rot ro roo rit raren," Art pleaded, trying to say, "Mr. Flogger, please don't flog me, I promise not to do it again."

"Oh I'm sure you won't do it again Art, I'm actually one hundred percent sure that you won't do it again," Mr. Flogger said. "But what I'm about to do to you here today will insure that you don't do it again. And even if you don't do it again I will want you back here for repeats of the session you're about to endure."

"RHATTT?" Art reeled, trying to say "WHAT?"

"Well you wouldn't want me shirking my duties by *not* keeping you in line and well-paced would you Art?" Mr. Flogger chuckled. "You would be amazed at how many young men come here to be disciplined for offenses they haven't even committed, just thought about, yes, you would be amazed indeed."

When the dean was shirtless Art found that his cock was engorging even more. The college student never defined himself as gay, but the sight of that well-toned chest, the big nipples and washboard stomach, the muscular arms and shoulders spoke to the dean's own discipline... Obviously the discipline he heaped on himself to keep himself in tip-top USMC corp. shape... OOH RAH...

"Shall we begin, Art?" Mr. Flogger asked as he undid the button on his slacks.

Before Art could respond the dean took the flogger from between the college boy's teeth and WHAPPED him hard three times across his hairless chest, the sound of the flogger's leather ends connecting with his skin maddening and the feeling totally hot and stinging.

"OWWW. OH GOD, OH MY FUCKING GOD!" Art bellowed. "That flogger hurts, Mr. Flogger!"

"Of course it hurts, Art, how else would you learn a lesson if it didn't hurt?" the dean asked, sounding to Art as if he were the dumbest college student on earth.

With that, Mr. Flogger raised the implement and thrashed Art five more times across the chest, the handsome college student doing his best to stay perched and balanced atop the piles of encyclopedias.

"RRRHHH!" Art cried through clenched teeth. "Mr. Flogger, Sir, what if people passing in the hallway outside hear me?"

The dean laughed again and said, "No worries on that Art, no worries on that at all." And with that he flogged the college student another five thrashes across his chest, this time making sure to really connect with Art's jutted up nipples.

"AWWWHHH, God that smarts," Art reeled pitifully.

"Do you think you'll be cheating again any time soon on any tests, Art?" Mr. Flogger asked.

"NO, no Sir, I will never cheat again Mr. Flogger," Art sputtered, his head down, his teeth clenched and taking in the sight of his reddening chest.

The next time the dean WHAPPED Art's chest with the flogger the student noticed that the dean was now holding his own hard cock in one hand... and used the other hand to swing the flogger... and he administered another ten WHAPS to the young man's chest.

"AWWWHHH, HHHUUUHHH, OH FUCK Mr. Flogger, Sir!" Art bellowed, looking up at the ceiling now as he cried out. "Burning man, my chest and my poor tits are burning up Sir..."

"Will you again cheat on one of Mr. Goldberg's tests?" the dean asked and whapped the college student again five times HARD across the chest with the flogger.

"FUUUCCCKKK, no, definitely not, not on Mr. Goldberg's tests or any other instructor Mr. Flogger, Sir," Art seethed.

"But especially not Mr. Goldberg's tests, right Art?" Mr. Flogger asked and began making his way behind the bound up perched college student.

From the mocking sound of the question that Mr. Flogger had just asked him it was obvious that the dean knew he was sucking Mr. Goldberg's cock to insure his passing grades. Oh what a cruel twist of fate this was Art thought.

Here he was sucking cock like a faggot to insure good grades and when the instructor catches him cheating he turns him in, go figure...

Suddenly, Art's thoughts were cut short as the dean stood behind him, swung his flogger and whapped him hard a few times in succession across his melon-shaped ass globes.

"YOWWW!" Art screamed and squiggled around a bit atop the encyclopedias.

"Stay in place Art, if you fall from those encyclopedias I'll begin this discipline session all over again," Mr. Flogger said, raised the instrument of Art's torture and whaled into his ass cheeks ten times in HARD stinging succession.

"OWWWHHH, OHHHUUUHHH, y-yes Mr. Flogger, I'll stay in place, I don't want any more than what I deserve for cheating on Mr. Goldberg's test," Art cried out, not believing himself the quibble that was coming out of his mouth.

"Good man Art, I see you've accepted that what you're being dealt here today is worth every moment of your time," the dean said, raised his flogger and again WHAPPED the young man's rear end ten more times.

"AYYY!" Art screamed in response.

"H-how much more of this do you plan to do to me Mr. Flogger?" Art asked.

"HEH, when I'm done flogging you I'm going to paddle you young man," Mr. Flogger said and again, Art's jaw dropped.

"P-paddle me? Mr. Flogger, trust me on this, I'm learning a hard lesson here from being flogged, and you don't need to paddle me too!" Art reeled and in response Mr. Flogger WHAPPED him another ten flogs across his butt cheeks. "AYYYRRR, GODDD!"

Then, as the dean WHAPPED and WHAPPED his ass cheeks harder and harder the young college student found himself dancing precariously around and when he hopped over to one stack of the encyclopedias Mr. Flogger whaled into him all the more, for not following instructions he stated harshly.

"OH PLEASE Mr. Flogger, my ass feels hot enough to fry an egg on!" Art bawled miserably.

"HMMM, that's a good idea Art, maybe I'll send you to the cooking shop after this and see if that's possible," Mr. Flogger said with a grin and as Art now balanced himself miserably on one stack of the encyclopedias the dean WHAPPED and WHAPPED and WHAPPED his butt cheeks with the flogger.

The young man also could not help noticing just how hard the dean's cock was at that point as it stuck out of the top of his slacks...

"Obviously this is a rush for him," Art said to himself.

"OH and I should mention that when we get to the paddling end of your discipline session Art, I have to hope that you REALLY like being trussed up, more than you are at the moment," the dean stated laughingly.

"WHAT?" Art reeled as Mr. Flogger flogged his butt cheeks some more.

"Trust me young man, it's for your own good, as all of this here today is, for your own good that is," Mr. Flogger said teasingly then... and it was at that point that Art knew that this was a sexual rush for the ex-marine.

The college student had heard stories of marines who purposely endured tests of their strength and mettle and how it aroused them in the cock, even if they weren't gay, and obviously Mr. Flogger had been just such a marine, even though he was presently at the other end of the endurance test that was being meted out... Obviously he was a marine who thrived on dishing it out...

When Art's ass cheeks were crimson, striped and welted as well Mr. Flogger stepped to the front of the young man, gave his chest and nipples a few final WHAPPING flogs and then in a fast motion cut him down from the ropes with a knife from his slacks' pocket...

"OWWW, OWWW, HUUUHHH," Art panted, cried and gasped as he slid to the floor and lay there in a heap at Mr. Flogger's feet.

"I'll give you a few moments to collect yourself Art, and then you're going to be paddled," Mr. Flogger said, standing and looming directly over his young charge.

To Mr. Flogger's shock and total surprise Art reached forward and with his hands trembling he grabbed the dean's ankles around his slacks and pressed his lips against one of his shoes. He pressed hard kisses against Mr. Flogger's shoes as he cried and cried his red ass in the air, his chest and nipples stinging and burning... and there was still more to come...

Chapter 3

A short while later, Art Riley found himself trussed up tight at the upper body, his arms pinned behind him and his wrists cinched securely as well... The way Mr. Flogger had tied him showed off the muscles he had attained while weight lifting and the dean it seemed had purposely made a showcase of the young man's nipples...

Mr. Flogger, him also naked now as the day he was born and using the young college student's reddened ass to guide him with, brought him over to what he had deemed the spanking chair...

"Oh GAWWWD Mr. Flogger, is this really necessary Sir?" Art moaned miserably as the dean held his much wounded ass cheek tight and meanly.

"Very necessary Art," the dean replied. "And if you ask one more stupid question like that I'll re-flog your ass and chest after I'm done paddling you now."

With that Mr. Flogger hauled the young man over his lap, rubbed his stinging butt cheeks a few times with his rectangular shaped wooden paddle... and then raised it high, and brought it crashing down HARD on Art's poor butt cheeks...

"OWWW!" Art screamed anew... realizing also that the dean had put him in a position so that his hard cock was pressed against his leg.

"GOD, he's making my hard cock rub against his massive thigh as he swats me now with a goddamned wooden paddle, a fraternity paddle no doubt," Art reeled inwardly. "Fucking pervert ex-marine is going to make me cum, oh fuck, this is humiliating!"

The sounds of the wooden paddle now connecting with the bare flesh of Art Riley's ass cheeks filled the room, along with the scents of man sweat and pain, anguish and debasement... if those things had a scent that is...

As Mr. Flogger Paddled and swatted Art's ass cheeks he tugged on the upper ropes binding the young man tight... and rocked him up and down and up and down against his upper thigh...

"HUUUHHH Mr. Flogger, why, why is my cock so hard and worked up?" Art asked, sounding dense and totally tormented.

"It means you're realizing that what I'm doing to you here today is very much worth it all Art," Mr. Flogger said, tugged the ropes harder, paddled the young man harder and then it happened...

"YUHHH, FUUUCCCKKK Mr. Flogger, I'm cumming, fuck, I'm in such pain here but I'm cumming, unthinkable, but so hot..." Art panted as he was relentlessly paddled, shooting his load at the same time all over Mr. Flogger's thigh.

"That's it Art, let it happen, don't overthink it, just let it happen," Art heard Mr. Flogger saying as if from far away at that point...

After the young man's ass was as red as a fire engine Mr. Flogger stopped paddling him, helped him off his lap and switched places with him, sitting the still tied up Art Riley in the chair...

When Art looked up at the dean standing over him he said, "WH-when did you get dressed again Mr. Flogger?"

Cupping the young man's chin in his hand and tilting his head back the dean said smiled and said, "I move a lot faster than you can ever realize Art..."

That said the dean leaned down and pressed his lips hard against the college students...

"Be here a week from today for another discipline session young man," the dean ordered as he began untying Art.

"Y-yes Sir," Art Riley said, feeling his cock engorging yet again...

The End

Thinking of Master Jeff...

Family Picnic Gone Awry

A Kidnap Fantasy Fetish Story

I had been working six-day weeks at my job as a banking vice president, nearly twelve to fourteen hours a day. When I finally got an entire weekend off my wife insisted that we all take a day together and go, as a family, on a picnic to the beautiful area known as "Mont Park" a few miles from where we live in the suburbs. To be honest I totally agreed with her, that she and I and our two kids, our twelve-year-old son and eight-year-old daughter *needed* a family day out... and "Mont Park" was the perfect setting for it. "Mont Park" boasts beautiful towering trees, freshly mowed grass for two to three miles at a stretch, a built-in swimming pool, the cleanest public restrooms a family could ask for... and a fine area for picnicking.

So, at my wife's suggestion we packed up three picnic baskets with sandwiches, cold drinks, desserts and a fourth basket held three big tablecloths that we would use to spread our picnic out on. We left the house at eleven AM (in my case, it would be the last time I ever left the house or saw my family) that Saturday morning and drove to "Mont Park." It was a nearly two hour drive, given that we hit hordes of traffic nearly every step of the way, AND, I had drunk nearly three large cups of coffee that morning... so by the time we arrived at "Mont Park", found a parking spot in the public lot and unloaded our picnic gear from the trunk of the car I had to piss like a racehorse, as we macho so-and-so's call it when the need to relieve ourselves is at the boiling point.

After we had unpacked the picnic gear I told my family to wait for me by the car, saying that I was going to quickly dash over to the public restroom, relieve myself and that I would be back in a jiffy… and from there we would find a nice spot for our picnic. My twelve-year-old son laughed and said, "Man, Daddy always has to pee like so bad while the rest of us can wait all day."

I chuckled at my son's observation and then dressed in a pair of navy blue cargo shorts a white and gray pique polo shirt and brown lace-up dock shoes with no socks I dashed as quickly as my feet would take me to the men's room of "Mont Park." As I hurried along the need to piss increased more and more and I had to laugh at the fact that the damned public bathrooms had to be so far from the parking lot.

But finally, oh blessed finally, I made it to the men's public restroom and quickly made my way up to one of the urinals. Dancing stupidly and teetering and tottering from foot to foot I managed to extract my cock from my shorts and breathed sigh after sigh of relief as I began trickling and yeah, flooding my yellow stream into the urinal.

As I was pissing and pissing like the proverbial racehorse I mentioned earlier two guys, one an older looking dude dressed all in black, black slacks, black button down shirt and even a black silk tie (dressed like that in a picnic park?) and a younger dude, him dressed in fatigue style pants and an olive colored tee shirt with dog tags dangling around his neck (I guessed him to be a solider boy or maybe even a marine) sidled up to the urinals on either side of me.

"Feels good to relieve yourself huh son?" the older dude asked me as we three stood there lined up at the urinals, us three being the only dudes in the bathroom at that moment, sadly for me.

"Yeah, sure as hell it does at that, but if you don't mind bud, I really don't like chatting with anyone while I'm pissing and especially while I got my cock in my hand, no offense okay?" I replied to the older guy.

Glancing over at him I saw that he was smiling evilly... and I also saw that he WAS NOT taking a leak. As I went on pissing, it seemed that it would never end, damned coffee; I glanced over at the younger dude on the other side of me and saw that he too was not pissing. These two dudes were simply standing at my sides, *watching me piss, JEEZ, oh FUCKING JEEZ!*

"Hey you two, what gives here?" I barked as the last trickles of my mess spurted from my semi hard cock. "Never saw a dude piss before?"

As I was packing my cock back into my shorts and was about to zip up the dude dressed in the fatigues gear stepped away from the urinal he was at, stepped behind me and punched me HARD, FUCKING HARD across the back of my head.

"ARRRHHH!" I roared in a man's pain and all six feet and musculature of me landed in a heap on the men's room floor in front of the urinal I had just deposited my offering in.

In a stupor and with my head pounding I felt myself lifted from the floor from under my arms and at my ankles and lugged out of the back entrance of the men's public restroom...

Sometime later, don't ask me how much later I found myself in what appeared to be a garage of some sort, but lo and fucking behold it was set up like a makeshift filming studio as there were cameras and spotlights and tripods set up all over the fucking place. To add insult to injury I was stripped totally naked AND tied up tight at the upper torso, my tits showcased real nice let me tell you, and my cock and balls tied up to... and balanced on my knees atop two heavy-duty wooden boxes, my feet tied to the boxes, FUCK!

I screamed and roared in total terror, I mean, who wouldn't in my place? I had just been literally kidnapped and carried off, *taken from my family*... but for what? FOR WHAT? Why was I in some sort of filming studio AND why was I tied the fuck up and naked as the day I was born?

As I steadied myself atop those wooden boxes, the two dudes who had snagged me out of the public restroom sidled up at my sides... and began inspecting me as if I were merchandise of some sort...

They reached under me and tweaked my nipples, twisted them, pinched the fucking fucks out of them and mashed them good and hard.

"AYYYRRR!" What do you fucking fucked up dudes want with me?" I roared, my head still hurting from the blow it had been dealt and hanging down a bit as I was handled like some sort of product. "I'm a family man and my family is waiting for me at Mont Park right now!"

"HEH, well, sorry to tell you family man, but your family is very, very far away from you at the moment," the older man said as he next stepped behind me and trailed his thin delicate but claw-like fingers down my tied up cock shaft and over my big golf-ball sized testicles as they hung embarrassingly behind me between my muscular thighs. "You know what, that will be a good title for the flicks we'll star you in, "Family Man."

"What in all hell does that mean? *Star me in?* I didn't come to Mont Park to be turned into a goddamned movie star for faggot porn, and stop fingering my goods back there, huh Mister?" I bitched.

As the older man played with my family jewels and cock behind me his young cohort stood next to me, still reaching under me and tweaking and kneading my nipples, even squeezing and tugging on my muscular man breasts.

"Sure thing Boss man, he's perfect for the flicks we're gonna make, when he bitches and moans it'll make the productions all the more real," the young guy said to the older man as he too handled me. "I can't believe we got so lucky so early in the day when we decided to scope out Mont Park for a mark..."

"Yes, and we will rake in millions with this "family man", the older man said and then to my utter shock and astonishment I felt his fingers diddling their way into my manhole.

"HEYYY! NO! NO! OH NO! Don't be violating my asshole you scumbag!" I bellowed angrily and in terror, the fact that I had been kidnapped for the reason of being made into an unwilling porn star setting in hard and heavy.

And fuck me hard buds, as the older man diddled my asshole and played my cock and testicles like they were musical instruments with his other hand and as his young cohort teased my nipples and man breasts, OH MY FUCKING GOD, but my tied cock betrayed me by getting all hard and steely... and being that my poor cock was tied up the way it was I laid what was a real painful hard-on.

"*And there it is*, the erection I was waiting for," the older man said from behind me.

The next thing I felt was the needle tip of a syringe being injected into one of the thick veins of my cock shaft. I screamed in a mixture of pain and terror, roaring about how I was not a drug user and what the fuck was that that they were injecting into me? AND into my poor cock at that?

The older man said that it was just a good dose of Viagra and some minerals and vitamins from the Orient... adding that it would keep me good and fucking erect for my debut, which was about to happen in the next few minutes...

When he was done emptying the syringe into the vein in my cock shaft the young guy dressed in military garb grinned meanly at me and curled one hand into a big fist.

"AWWW NO, NO, not again you scumbag mug!" I blathered, but he ignored me and punched me again atop the head.

I went careening off the two boxes the men had balanced me on, hit the floor in a heap and as unconsciousness took me a second time that day I saw a few more men entering the garage we were in... my fucking co-stars as I would soon learn...

A short while later, when I was again conscious I found myself tied up in a new position... and starring in my first segment of what would be a series of videos titled "Family Man." My co-stars had a blast using me and I found out later as well that all of them were on the older man's payroll, as he was the owner of the video production company, as for me, I was just an extra... and definitely not on the payroll...

As time went on I wondered about my wife and kids... and wondered if I was being searched for by the authorities. I was a pretty high paid banking executive after all, but then, when one of my co-stars told me that we weren't even in the United States I knew why no mention of my having been so brutally kidnapped and turned into a porn star had made the news... What a family picnic gone awry huh?

The End

Thinking of my muse, John Robinson...

Dad's Feet

A Male Foot Fetish Story

"I have to tell you Shawn, it sure was great of you to invite us over here tonight to watch the football game with you and your dad," Dean said as he and Evan entered their work buddy, Shawn's three bedroom condo after work that Friday night in the bank they all worked for.

All three of the twenty-something year old young men were in their suits with their ties pulled down a few notches and the first few buttons of their dress shirts unbuttoned, evidence of the exhaustion and stress they had endured during the last few days.

"Yeah, I figured after all the talk during the past nutty week about the game and after all the beer and chips and pretzels and cigars I had stockpiled I would have you guys over," Shawn said as he closed and locked the condo door. "Besides, working twelve hour days I think merits us dudes a nice relaxing Friday night before the weekend."

"Well, I couldn't agree with you more bud, and with all the football game supplies you bought and with all that me and Dean have here we'll really make it an evening with you and your dad," Evan said, holding up a large canvas shopping bag, which was filled with bags of pretzels, chips, a twelve pack of cold beer and extra cigars. "How long is your dad staying with you anyway?"

"Just until Sunday, then he heads back to Washington, he needed to have some in-person meetings with the managers of some of the branches here in New York for the company he works for," Shawn said, shucking off his suit jacket and hanging it in a closet. "You guys can hang your suit jackets in here, I have plenty of hangers."

"Thanks man," Dean said as he and Evan took off their suit jackets as well and hung them up.

"You guys get comfortable on the couch, turn on the TV, the remote is there on the coffee table, I'll go get everything ready we'll need in the kitchen," Shawn said, picking up the large canvas shopping bag from where Evan had placed it on the floor of the living room. "There are also a few ashtrays if you want to light up some cigars. Can't hurt to smoke some victory cigars before the game starts, may bring our team luck at that."

"You want some help out there in the kitchen bud?" Dean asked undoing the knot in his tie and letting it dangle down the sides of his white button down shirt.

"NAH, I got it under control," Shawn said with a grin. "Besides, you know how anal I am when it comes to preparing stuff."

At that the three young men laughed good-naturedly and watched as Shawn, his brown hair cut in the style of a true banker sauntered into the kitchen.

"Hey, where's your dad?" Evan called out to Shawn. "I thought he was going to be watching the game with us."

Shawn stuck his head out of the kitchen door and said, "More than likely in his room, I set up the third bedroom as a guest room. Lucky him, unlike us slaves to the bank's upper management he doesn't have to work overtime, just goes to his meetings and then comes home."

"You want us to go and let him know we're here?" Dean asked.

Shawn grinned his killer smile, his brown eyes lighting up as he did so and said, "Damn, you two really are anxious to help out huh?"

"It's the least we can do," Dean said, running a hand through his short-cropped black hair.

"Okay, go ahead, let him know we're here," Shawn said. "Third room down the hall.

Knowing that father of mine he's probably out cold napping. If he heard us come in he would have been out here already and said hello. When he naps he doesn't hear shit, totally sleeps like the dead. Always wished I could be like that but I wake up at the slightest sound. My mother has told me over the years of the times where she had to wake him up to get ready for work and he *still* slept right through her nudging and prodding him."

Evan smiled wide, his blue eyes gleaming, said, "Yeah, I sleep like that too at times," and then he and Dean walked from the living room down the hallway Shawn had indicated toward the guest room.

When the two young bankers got to the guest bedroom they saw that the door was slightly ajar.

"Mr. Sommers?" Dean said softly and tapped on the door with one knuckle.

When he didn't hear a response Dean looked at Evan and they both shrugged. Evan gave the door a slight nudge, revealing that the light in the room was on.

"Okay, the room is totally lit up so he must be in there," Evan said.

"Mr. Sommers?" Dean said again and as he pushed the door open some more he and Evan stepped into the well-lit beautifully furnished room.

"Damn, nice, real nice," Evan said. "Shawn has awesome decorating taste. He'll make some girl a good husband someday..."

The two young men looked across the room and saw that the bed was empty, but upon further inspection they saw that the couch that was set up on the other side of the room was definitely not empty, because that's where Shawn's father was, sleeping and snoring softly as he did so. The man was still wearing his shirt and tie, suit pants and black dress socks, his shoes on the floor in front of the couch.

"Ah, there he is," Dean said softly and closed the door behind them. "Just as Shawn said, napping."

Dean and Evan made their way quietly over to the couch where the well-dressed man was sleeping, but then, when they were a few feet (feet being the keyword here) Evan stopped short and seemed to gasp.

"Oh Jesus," Evan said, stopping cold in his tracks.

"What is it bud? What's wrong?" Dean asked, grabbing Evan by his upper arm and holding it tight. "You okay man? You, you're shaking."

"Fuck me hard man, look, look at Mr. Sommers' feet, fucking fuck man, look at his feet in those thin black nylon dress socks," Evan said softly. "Look at how they're shaped, look at those arches, look at the outline of those toes of his. Goddamn, look at his feet, *look at his feet.*"

As Evan spoke he was stepping to the end of the couch where Shawn's father was obviously fast asleep and totally unaware of the presence of his son's two work buddies.

"Man, what are you going on about the man's socked feet for?" Dean asked, letting go of Evan's arm as they both now stood over where Shawn's father's dress socked shapely tootsies were dangling off the end of the couch.

"Do like I said, look at them, *really look* at those feet of his bud, they must be at least size eleven or twelve," Evan said, sounding as if he couldn't breathe properly, his lips trembling as he spoke. "Fucking look at his feet, oh God..."

"Dude, they're just feet, a guy's feet in dress socks, they're our buddy Shawn's dad's feet in dress socks," Dean said. "Okay, I'll agree with you, they are more than likely size eleven or twelve or so, they are nicely shaped, he has nice arches and yeah, his toes are really outlined in them, which means he must have really pounded the pavement in his shoes and really sweated... and..."

The two young men looked at each other for a second and then back down at the man's socked feet as they dangled off the end of the couch...

"Jesus, you're right, and they smell great too, all leathery and silk mixed together with a guy's feet sweat, what's up with that Evan?" Dean asked, tugging on one of the ends of his dangling tie, he too breathless now it seemed, AND he feeling the beginnings of a definite erection in his suit trousers.

"Yeah, he must have really pounded the pavement in his shoes and socks today," Evan said, his hands trembling as he slowly made his way down to his knees in front of Shawn's father's dangling socked feet. "That would explain the scent emanating from them."

With that, Dean watched in awe, amazement and total shock as well, as his buddy positioned his nose scant inches from the sleeping man's socked toes and sniffed heartily.

"AW man, fucking pungent, real spicy Mr. Sommers' socks smell," Evan whispered, his voice cracking as he again stole more sniffs at the man's socked toes, a look of ecstasy on his handsome face.

"Damn Evan, what in all hell are you doing here?" Dean rasped through clenched teeth. "You're sniffing Shawn's father's damned toes."

"His *socked* toes Dean and they smell wonderful," Evan said and then moved his nose along the sleeping man's side of his foot, sniffing and inhaling deeply as he went. "Oh man, the aroma is intoxicating bud."

With a look of sheer astonishment on his face Dean lowered himself slowly to his knees next to Evan, at Shawn's fathers other dangling socked foot.

Without thinking about it he pressed his nose against the smooth bottom of the man's socked foot and stuck out his tongue. As Evan continued to sniff at Shawn's fathers toes on one foot Dean trailed his tongue along the bottom of the other one, sniffing as well as he went along.

"Fuck, his socks taste real good somehow," Dean said, tears forming in his eyes. "I can't believe we're doing this Evan... Evan?"

When Dean looked at his buddy he saw that Evan had his nose buried in the arch of the sleeping man's other foot and he was grinning devilishly.

"Shawn was right, his father sleeps like he's dead," Evan said, lifting his face momentarily away from the arch of the man's foot.

"Yeah, for sure that bud, and while he's sleeping *we're* licking and sniffing his damned smelly dress socked tootsies," Dean said.

"That and then some bud," Evan said and sidled to the end of the couch on his knees, so that Mr. Sommers' feet were staring him in the face.

"What's up with this man? Why, *why* in all hell are we doing this, sniffing and licking and then some to this man's socked feet?" Dean asked Evan.

Evan wrapped his fingers of both hands around the balls of one of Mr. Sommers' socked feet, squeezed it a bit, looked to his side at Dean and said, "Dude, don't overthink it, just do it. LOTS of guys fantasize about shit like this, but they don't talk about it. Just do it, like the saying goes, *just do it*..."

That said, Evan stuck out his tongue and trailed it up and down and up and down the bottom of Mr. Sommers' foot as he held it tight in his fingers.

"OH sweet, sweet heaven," Evan said, sounding almost like he was crying.

Dean then did the same thing, grabbed Mr. Sommers' balls of his other foot with his fingers, held them tight, stuck out his tongue and began licking the bottom of the man's socked foot up and down and up and down...

"JEEZ, I can't believe we're doing this, licking the socked feet of our bud's father," Dean said and then pressed his lips HARD against the man's socked heel and kissed it, kissed it, and kissed it.

"Fuck, yeah, I have to admit I always wondered about dudes in dress socks, I mean, I never wondered about me in my dress socks, but other dudes, you know Evan?" Dean asked and then squeezed Mr. Sommers' toes in his fingers, massaging them, kneading them.

"Yeah, I know what you mean bud, it's one of the mysteries of the universe," Evan chuckled and then watched as Dean hoisted the sleeping man's foot by his toes and wrapped his lips around those socked toes... and sucked hard, sucked as if he was sucking in the very essence of life.

Dean's eyes were closed in ecstasy as he sucked the juice from Mr. Sommers' socked toes...

Evan simply smiled and followed his buddies lead, hoisted Mr. Sommer's foot up by the socked ankle and gobbled his socked toes into his mouth.

As the two men sucked heartily at the man's socked toes they caressed his socked calves, and as they did so, he began to stir on the couch...

"HHHRRRMMM... aww, whass-what's goin' on at my feet eh? That shit, whatever *that is*, it feels real nice... awww man, feels like my feet are bein' licked and sucked on, what..." Mr. Sommers said as he pressed a hand over his eyes to get the sleep dust out...

He heard the sound of a door closing, opened his eyes and when he sat up on the couch he looked down and saw that his socks appeared to have been pulled down a bit, as they were scrunched around his muscular and shapely calves...

"What the fuck just went on here?" he said with a look of bemusement on his handsome face...

A short while later Shawn, Dean and Evan... and Shawn's dad were all sitting in the living room. They were sipping mugs of beer, smoking cigars and munching on pretzels and chips while watching the football game...

And as they watched the game, as Dean and Evan sat next to each other on the couch, Mr. Sommers had his socked feet propped in their laps...

"I don't know why you boys scurried out of my room so fast," Mr. Sommers said as each of the young men massaged one of his socked feet each, and even held them aloft to lick and suck at them in between massaging them. "I for one just love having my feet worked on. I have office boys back in Washington who can't get enough of my feet, with my damned socks on at that..."

"Yeah, I wonder why," Evan said jokingly and lifted Mr. Sommers' foot to his mouth and planted a few delicate kisses on it.

"And Shawn knows all about it, don't you son?" Mr. Sommers' asked his son, who was seated nearby in a living room chair.

"Yeah, always took care of my dad's socks for him when I lived at home," Shawn replied and puffed on his cigar, grinning, watching as his two buddies took care of his dad's tootsies, glad that he had invited them over... and somehow having known how the evening would turn out...

The End

Thinking of Tony N. Trainer...

Soldier Boy McCann

A Military/Milking Fetish Story

It shouldn't happen to a soldier, FUCK, it shouldn't happen to *any* man what the fuck happened to me... AND all because I had to take an all time over the top racehorse sized piss, nothing unusual there for a guy. A soldier or any man for that matter should be able to walk into a bar, use their facilities and not, I repeat, NOT be accosted in humiliating, sexual ways...

And he also shouldn't have to endure drinking his and other men's piss out of used urinals OR having his scalp shaved down to goddamned peach fuzz... but sadly... and maddeningly all those things and more, AND MORE, happened to me, good old twenty-seven year old army Sergeant Peter McCann... and like I said, all because I needed to take a marine-sized piss. HA, you gotta love my twisted sense of humor there, a soldier boy taking a marine-sized piss.

Anyway, you're probably wondering what the fucking fuck I'm going on about here, well, it happened a few weeks ago at this point... and even though I survived it, thank God for the mental end of military training... but even though I survived it I still have dreams and flashbacks of it, typical reactions for a military man, and lo and fucking behold, every time I either dream about it or remember it my huge horse-sized cock plumps up all hard and firm and aches to cum... and cum I do... FUCK!

And fucking how like I said, it was a few weeks ago at this point that it happened... right after the Memorial Day weekend no less, JEEZ, talk about twisted turns of events and cruel irony. Talk about the injustices of injustices. I had spent the three-day weekend in upstate New York, visiting with my family at my parent's house. Cousins, aunts and uncles and even my grandparents were all there, it was a great time and a great way to spend Memorial Day weekend.

I can't tell you just how very proud my parents were to see me when I arrived all decked out in my olive colored dress uniform, complete with spit-shined lace-up patent leather shoes. Being their only child it really gives them a sense of pride to see me in my military gear. The reason I mention this is because I love being in the army... it was something I had wanted to do since I was old enough to remember... but I prefer the more casual khakis and fatigues we soldier boys wear as opposed to the more dressy uniform... and it was when I was in my goddamned fatigues on the night that I was driving home after the long weekend spent with my family that my agony occurred.

On Sunday afternoon of the Memorial Day weekend the family gathered once more at my parent's house and we all spent the day together, not knowing when we would be able to all see each other like this again. Given the state of the world the way it is lately no one knows for sure *where* a soldier can be deployed to, JEEZ! So without really giving it much thought I suppose it can be said that I drank a lot more soft drinks than I realized. Sitting out in the sun will cause a lot of people to do that, especially while sitting around talking and reminiscing. I hadn't touched any alcohol that Sunday, seeing as I would be driving back to my base, Fort Kensington, in Brooklyn New York, at least a five to six hour drive.

After the emotional good-byes and promises to all see each other again real soon, my relatives advising me to stay safe and how they would pray that I didn't get deployed to any war-torn countries I packed my one big luggage and duffel bag into the trunk of my car and headed back toward my base. It was around eight PM when I left my parent's home, looking in the rearview mirror as everyone waved at me. With a few tears in my eyes I watched in the rearview till I couldn't see anyone back there anymore. Dressed comfortably in my beige colored fatigues and black combat boots I pressed my foot to the gas pedal and headed for the parkway.

It was about an hour and a half to two hours into my drive that I found myself squirming a bit, the need to piss suddenly kicking in solid and heavy... and fuck me hard man, it seemed that the traffic I had hit was causing me to back up in time. I figured at this rate that it would take me more than five or six hours to get back to my base, it would take at least eight to ten hours at this speed. I had plenty of gas that wasn't the problem. The problem was, like most guys out there I stupidly didn't have a bottle or container to piss my stream into for emergencies such as this one... JEEZ! As I drove at a slower than the speed limit speed I found myself curling my toes back in my thick army issued beige colored socks in my boots, that's how fucking bad I was starting to have to piss.

Looking up at the signs above the parkway I saw that the next exit was half a mile off. I had no choice, I had to get off the goddamned parkway and find a place where I could relieve myself. I maneuvered my car into the exit lane and moments later I found myself in a deserted area that was surrounded mostly by woods.

"Jeez, of all the exits to get off at I had to choose that one," I said, glancing down at the bulge in my fatigue pants, which was my piss-filled erection.

I drove about a half-mile or so and then I found it, a bar with a neon sign that proclaimed its name to be "The Local." It was the only place around so I really had no goddamned choice in the matter I suppose it could be said. There was a small parking lot in the back of the place where a good amount of cars were parked. Even though the place was all by itself in a lonely deserted area, it appeared, and based on the amount of parked cars I saw that a lot of people knew about the place. Never once did I figure that it was some sort of sleazy establishment, the need to piss was past the boiling point AND that was all I could think about at that moment.

I quickly found a spot in the parking lot, turned off the car's ignition ad stepped out. I took a quick look around and thought how I could easily have just taken a whiz in the woods on the roadside. But with my luck there would be a state trooper or two lurking somewhere nearby, just looking for a reason to arrest a handsome soldier boy in his fatigues and combat boots.

Nah, better just to play it safe and piss in the bathroom of the bar I had found... RIGHT!

I walked quickly through the parking lot to the front door of "The Local", stepped inside the dimly lit establishment and was greeted with clouds of cigar, cigarette and even marijuana fumes. To the right of the entrance was the main bar, which stretched all the way to the other end of the establishment. It looked, from where I was standing, that every stool at the bar was occupied... *by men only*. Try as I may I didn't see any women in the place. Across from the bar, behind a waist-high partition was a seating area.

The men were dressed in suits and ties, jeans with tee shirts and boots or sneakers, leather gear and some guys were even dressed in cowboy attire. They sat at the tables with drinks in front of them, some of them smoking cigars, some smoking cigarettes and some sharing fat marijuana joints. Jeez, they were smoking weed and I had been worried about being arrested for pissing in the woods? HA, ha, ha and HAR, HAR on me huh buds? I had to wonder though why on a weekend night some of the men at "The Local" would be dressed in business attire, more than likely men on business trips having a late-night drink with their buddies... or making new business buddies to drink with... and whatever else they fancied... JEEZ.

As I looked around for where the men's room might be it was not lost on me how I was being scrutinized by some of the patrons of "The Local." It was obvious that this was some sort of sleazy fetish type bar, given how some of the men were attired. I figured that in my military gear of fatigues and combat boots I fit right in. But then again, maybe not, seeing as I appeared to be the only guy dressed as I was. I managed a smile and slowly made my way through the crowd at the bar, trying to get to the bare chested extra muscles man bartender.

"Excuse me Sir," I called out to the very hairy dark haired dark eyed muscleman behind the bar, trying to make myself heard over the din of raucous conversations of the men seated and standing around me.

One guy in particular, who appeared to be in his early to mid-fifties with salt and pepper colored hair, was standing a few feet away from me. He was wearing a REALLY expensive looking charcoal colored suit with a white shirt and a black tie...

... and with a drink in one hand he seemed to be literally drinking in the sight of me. I quickly looked away from him and again back at the bartender, who thankfully was now looking at me.

"What can I get for ya Soldier boy?" the bartender asked me in a deep baritone sounding voice, he also seeming to be leering hungrily at me.

"Uh, for the moment I really need to use your facilities Sir," I called out in reply. "If you require me to make a purchase I'll do so after I'm..."

"No worries Soldier boy, the bartender barked with a grin and pointed to the left of the bar, indicating a dimly lit corridor with a few doors on the left and right sides of it. "The bathroom, or as you military sorts call it, the latrine is right down that hallway, last door on the left."

"Much obliged Sir," I called back to the bartender and held out my hand to shake his.

He gripped my hand tight and yanked me a bit forward. Damn, the fucking guy was strong, good thing my boots were laced up nice and tight, because he might have heaved me right outa them, har, har, har for me buds and har, har, har for the poor bar patrons, because my feet and socks really get down to some serious stinking in my big combat boots.

"Thanks for all you do, *and will do* Soldier boy," the bartender said and then let go of my hand.

I told him he was welcome and turned to make my way to the men's room, my cock beyond piss hard and way past the goddamned boiling point by then. But as I was making my way politely through the crowd at the main bar, the guy in the charcoal colored suit was suddenly standing directly in front of me, his eyes, if they had mouths, literally devouring me, DAMN!

"May I help you Sir?" I asked the suit guy brusquely.

"When you're done relieving yourself in the latrine Soldier boy come on back here, any drink you want is on me," the guy said, leering at me and brazenly trailing a fingertip over my name patch on my fatigue shirt. "Soldier boy McCann…"

"That's Staff Sergeant McCann *Sir, and* while I thank you for your offer of a drink I really must be on my way… AFTER I have relieved myself that is!" I woofed at the guy and gently moved his hand away from my name patch, squeezing that hand in a threatening manner as I did so, showing him my soldier boy strength it could be said.

He seemed to get the message. And then, without another word I sauntered past the suit guy and made my way toward the hallway where the men's room was, passing a pool table as I went. I saw a group of sleazy looking skinheads all participating in a game of Pool. Some of them were white, some were black, some were Hispanic, but all of them were wearing sleeveless tees.

And FUCK, *all* of them were sporting gigantic, what looked like prison yard muscles. Their arms were adorned with all manner of tattoos and a couple of them who were shirtless had piercings in their nipples and tattoos all over their chests as well. I saw that some of them had piercings in their lips and noses as well. I had to wonder if any of them had piercings in their cocks as well, JEEZ.

But my attention was quickly averted away from the skinheads as the need to piss was becoming painful at that point. I hastened my step to the men's room.

As the bartender had said when he had directed me to the men's room and thanked me for all that I do and all that I would do (all that I would do? Why in all hell hadn't I heeded that cryptic warning and just bolted from the sleazy bar called "The Local?") the men's room was the last door on the left of the dimly lit hallway… the smell that was permeating the air around the door to the men's room was testament to that, YUK, YUK, YUK, as Curly of The Three Stooges used to say.

I pushed the door of the men's room open and was greeted by the sounds of a deep voice grunting and swearing from one of the stalls.

"FUCKERS, *goddamned bastards*, can't believe you guys put me through this shit again," and the guy who was swearing that way came shambling and staggering out of one of the stalls, bent over a bit as if he was in pain... and fuck me hard buds, but the guy was wearing just a pair of black calf length dress socks and his lace-up wingtips. "AND after Memorial Day Weekend at that... crappy thing to do to a former service man I got to say!"

From where I was standing I could see that his cock was pretty shriveled and used up, although even in its flaccid state it appeared to be a pretty impressively sized piece of man meat, a real thick and long sausage-shaped schlong... and his testicles were hanging down real low and used up looking as well in his sweaty sac, but like his cock, those testicles were of a notable size.

"And all because I got here early, thinking that the place wouldn't be all that crowded because of the Memorial Day Weekend, and maybe, JUST MAYBE, I could enjoy a few drinks, and maybe for a change meet someone of quality, BUT NO, you guys ambushed me again and made me into your endless cum font and meat market in that goddamned stall from hell," the guy was going on, all muscular and ripped in in just his socks and shoes, *what the fucking fuck*?

Standing by him were two guys, one of them blond and lanky, the other brown haired and really muscular looking but dopey looking at the same time. They were both dressed in jeans and tee shirts with sneakers... AND...

... the blond guy was holding a pair of suit pants and the brown haired guy was holding a white shirt and a suit jacket, obviously the clothing they were holding belonging to the naked but for his socks and shoes guy. As the guy grabbed his clothing from the two men he shouted in their faces, "And as usual I see that someone stole my goddamned underpants, FUCKERS, and they took the garters I was wearing as well, FUCK, every time, every fucking time I come here, why I don't call the cops on you I'll never know..."

As the guy grabbed the pants from the blond guy and quickly shucked himself into them over his shoes and socks the brown haired guy said, "But Mr. Smith, you know it's all in good but sleazy fun and..."

"YEAH, YEAH, fun shmun you muscles for brains bastard Ronald, in the meantime because of YOUR idea of *fun* my cock and balls are drained and useless for the next few days and my poor hole is gonna smart every time I shit for the next few days as well..." the guy said as he buttoned his suit pants and then grabbed his shirt and jacket from the blond guy. "Fuck, FUCK, some of those guys who rammed my back door didn't even have the decency to lube up, FUCK! And I would bet that you guys got the cops around here in your pockets as well, so what the fuck use would it be to report you two sleazy bar owners at that huh?"

In response the two men simply beamed manically at the guy as he next struggled himself into his white dress shirt. At that point he had turned around and I have to say that he was one handsome dark haired dark eyed mustached guy, looked like a real executive type at that. But what in all hell was he shouting and yelling at the two guys, who he had said were the bar owners, about?

As he stepped a bit more away from the stall he had come out of I saw piles of rope on the floor, JEEZ, what was that all about? Fuck that, had I been the smart soldier boy that I proclaimed myself to be I would have hightailed it out of that men's room *and* out of that bar at that moment.

"Where's my tie Alex?" the guy seethed in the blond bar owner's face.

"Sorry Greg, er, Mr. Smith, looks like when whoever whipped it off you when you were blindfolded with it took it, along with your cute underpants and garters that you had on tonight," Alex laughed meanly at the guy... who from what I could see from where I was standing could have easily broken the guy in half...

What in all hell was going on here anyway? Blindfolded with his tie? Took his underpants and garters? Who the fuck wore garters anymore?

As I listened to the ongoing tirade my cock pulsed in my fatigue pants and I had somehow forgotten that I had to piss the piss of a marine... even though I was a soldier boy... and while all this was going on between the stripped executive and the two bar owners men were sauntering in and out of the men's room like nothing was happening, except for the two guys dressed as cowboys who were making their way out of the men's room from the rear and meanly pinched the guy named Greg on his now suit pants covered ass.

"FUCKERS, bet you two were amongst the sleaze-bags that used me in here tonight huh?" the guy named Greg shouted at the two cowboys' backs as they looked back at him and wagged their tongues at him. "Did you guys suck my poor sore cock or fuck my damned bum? OR was it both sides of me that you fake cowboys partook of? Like I said, FUCKERS!"

With that, the handsome dude named Greg Smith haphazardly pulled on his suit jacket and trudged and stomped toward the door of the men's room... When he took notice of me standing there he said, "Great, now we have a dude dressed as a soldier here."

"*I am* a soldier Sir," I said to him, the scent of cum and piss emanating from the guy.

"So was I Sergeant McCann," Greg Smith said as he verified my stripes and name patch.

"And look what the fuck reward I got for it... milked and fucked beyond reason..."

Then, in what seemed like a flash he was gone, the men's room door slamming shut behind him. *Milked and fucked beyond reason? What in all hell did that mean?* When I turned and looked toward the stalls and row of urinals in the men's room my cock made the decision for me to get moving. If I didn't relieve myself now my fatigue pants would be a mess of piss.

I took a deep breath of the foul scented men's room air and made my way quickly up to one of the urinals on a back wall, passing by the two men who I had learned were the bar owners...

"And good evening to you Soldier boy," the blond guy said lustfully to me as I sidled up to a urinal between two other dudes who were pissing their brains out as well it seemed, one of them another suited guy and the other dressed in construction worker gear, total contrasts.

With my hands and fingers shaking a bit, that's how bad I needed to piss by then; I pulled down the zipper on my fatigue pants, reached in and extracted *my* giant schlong of a cock from the fly of my olive colored army issued briefs. I hung my cock over the urinal and began relieving myself.

"AWWW, FUCK, FUCK, yeah, really needed to take a marine sized piss!" I guttered loudly, stupidly and in a macho way.

I was standing nearly at attention as I did what I had to do, the sound of my frothy piss hitting the water of the urinal seeming to fill the air around me along with the other dudes who were also pissing on both sides of me.

"Such a shame that Mr. Smith had to leave so early tonight," I heard the dopey guy named Ronald saying from behind me; actually he sounded like he was *very close* behind me, GAWD!

"More of a shame that someone untied him, *or* that maybe he got himself untied this time, we'll have to be sure to tie him to the stall door good and REALLY tight next time," the guy named Alex said... and yes, the two men were by then standing directly behind me as I was pissing what felt like my guts out.

What in all fucks were these two clowns talking about... *tie a guy to a stall door*? What was up with that shit? FUCK me hard buds, but sadly for me I would soon find out... JEEZ!

"HAWWW, oh fuck, feels so good to be pissing at last," I mumbled stupidly as my stream seemed to be going on and on.

The two men who had been standing at my sides at the urinals were now zipping up, having finished their pissing business it seemed... but I couldn't help but notice that they hadn't flushed the urinals they'd just deposited their contributions in.

"Feels good to relieve yourself like that huh Soldier boy?" the guy named Alex asked me, and to my chagrin he was standing directly behind me, FUCK, I felt his jeans covered crotch rubbing up against my fatigue pants covered ass.

I didn't like the way the men at this establishment seemed to think that they could just take liberties with me, just because I was a soldier boy. That suited dude at the bar had fingered my nametag and now this guy was rubbing his damned crotch up against my ass, and FUCK, I could feel the fact that he was stacked up and hard in his pants, JEEZ!

"YEAH, but I'm not into talkin' to strangers while I'm doing my private business of pissing, makes me all nervous and sensitive feeling while I got my soldier sized cock in hand, AND what all do you think you're doing back there Sir?" I replied angrily. "I will thank you to remove yourself and your private area from *my* private area... I came into this establishment to relieve myself. I highly doubt that I am into the hijinks and escapades all of you are in this bar and..."

"HEH, HEH, talkin' to strangers he says," the big galloot of a guy named Ronald said from my side and just behind me. "Come on Soldier boy, don't you know that in life there's no such thing as strangers... we're all just buds that haven't met yet..."

"Very funny you are Sir," I replied, glancing quickly to the left, where Ronald was standing. "And ha, ha, for you."

As I was still pissing and pissing what felt like my guts out I was suddenly clocked hard on the top of my damned noggin, courtesy of the guy in the suit who had been pissing beside me.

"UUUHHHFFF!" I guttered, let go of my pissing cock and used both hands to steady myself over the urinal as I pressed my palms against the tile wall. "What the fuck fucker..."

But as I was ranting with my head spinning from the blow I'd just been dealt the construction worker who'd also been pissing beside me clocked me as well, right atop my old noggin too... making my peepers cross in my head.

"YUHHH!" I grunted this time... and found myself sliding and slithering to my knees in front of the urinal I had been pissing into, my cock still spurting beads of piss as I went.

"Good show, bloody good show!" I heard Alex chortle in a stupid sounding English accent as I landed in a semi-stupor, my face directly in front of the urinal, the smell of my piss filling my nostrils as my head spun some more.

As I sat there on my knees, the last of my piss emanating from my slit and splattering on my fatigue pants the dopey muscle head

Ronald reached down and the next thing I knew I was being relieved of my fatigue shirt. Fucking bruiser yanked my shirt up and over my shoulders and head and off me... JEEZ...

"HEY, what in all fucks do you think you're..." I began to protest but Alex quickly KPOWED me again atop my poor noggin. "YUHHHFFF!"

"And that's three lumps for your collection Soldier boy," Alex laughed as I found myself falling into darkness.

A few scant minutes later I came around a bit, the top of my head aching and pounding.

To my utter rage I found I had indeed been rendered shirtless, my massively muscular and ripped chest on total display... AND my shirt had been used to bind my wrists tightly behind me... GAWWWD!

"YARRRHHH! Oh you fucking bastards!" I roared as my face was forced into the urinal I had just filled with my frothy lemonade-like piss.

"Drink up Soldier boy, no one comes to the Local and doesn't drink!" Ronald said as he pushed my head deep into the urinal, until my nose and mouth were submerged it.

"AWWW!" I thundered into the urinal.

With no choice in the matter it seemed I stuck out my tongue and began lapping up and scoffing down my own rancid tasting piss.

"AWWW you lowlifes!" I panted as I pulled my head up to catch my breath in between drinking piss, *drinking piss, fuck, fuck, I was drinking MY piss,* OF ALL FUCKING THINGS.

"Finish up Soldier boy, we have two more urinals for you to clean out this way," Ronald said and meanly pushed my handsome face back into the damned urinal.

"UFFF!" I panted and once again slurped up my piss, fucking HUMILIATING!"

"And then after you're done it's into the milking stall for you, Alex chimed in.

The milking stall? As I heard those words I recalled what the guy named Greg Smith had said earlier before he stomped out of the place, how he had been tied to a stall door and drained AND fucked beyond belief! God almighty, what sort of sleazy place was this that fate had brought me to via my need to piss?

As I knelt there slurping and slopping up my piss I saw from the corners of my eyes men taking up position at the urinals next to me and pissing liberally into them. My heart sank when I heard Alex tell the men not to flush... *that I* would clean out the urinals.

At one point two other men, both of them in the garb of Leather men stood over me and pissed all over my head and onto my ripped and muscular back.

"Scum sucking bastards!" I reeled miserably, shaking my head from side to side as my short hair and face were soaked in piss.

It seemed that the two Leather men had a need each to piss more than I had to when I had entered the godforsaken establishment called The Local, because by the time they were done pissing on me, my head, hair and face were drenched with it. DAMN!

When the urinal that I had pissed into was completely emptied of my piss Ronald held my face in it just a tad longer... ordering me to use my tongue to clean the rims of the drain hole.

With tears of rage in my eyes I did the only thing I could think of in order to accomplish what Ronald had ordered me to do. I scoffed and hacked up some saliva, spit into the urinal a few times... and then used my tongue and my saliva as Windex to clean the rim of the drain hole in the urinal. From all around me I heard loud sounds of mocking macho laughter. I obviously had an audience at that point, GAWWWDD!

Then, when the urinal was cleaned to the satisfaction of my two sadistic captors they flushed it, making the cold water sluice all over my handsome mug of a face. I gratefully lapped up some of the cold water, trying to get the rancid taste of my piss out of my craw... and also glad that the cold water washed away some of the Leather men's piss.

Then, I was grabbed by my arms and still on my knees, moved to the left sided urinal next to the one I had pissed in and just finished cleaning. I was told to get busy slurping up the piss that was in that urinal. I clenched my tied up hands into a big fist, stuck out my tongue... and JEEZ Louise, I lowered my handsome mug into the frothy yellow mixture.

FUCKING two hours later I was done slopping down piss from the urinals. Two hours of slurping up and drinking down other men's piss, FUCCCKKK, for a soldier boy of my caliber it was beyond humiliating, it was downright de-fucking-grading. *My* piss had tasted bad enough let me tell you, but the piss of other men was beyond rancid. DAMN, I had been forced to slurp piss out of two more urinals tongue-wise... AND, by then my mouth was beyond rancid tasting and no matter how much water I scoffed down when the sadist bar owners flushed the urinals it did nothing to alleviate the taste of the mess in my poor craw. And what a sight that was let me tell you, drinking water from a flushing urinal, beyond demeaning buds.

Coughing and sputtering and spitting in a total soldierly rage I was then hauled up to my booted feet between Alex and Ronald.

"FUCKERS, what's the point of all this?" I gurgled loudly as Ronald held me tightly by one arm and Alex took me by the other. "Conk a soldier of my status *and* caliber into a snooze, strip him shirtless, tie him the fuck up with his own shirt and then make him clean out your rancid urinals with his tongue? UNACCEPTABLE I say, fucking UNACCEPTABLE! And to be pissed on by lowly lowlifes? EVEN more UN-FUCKING-ACCEPTABLE!"

"If you think all that was unacceptable Soldier boy wait till you see what you're in for next here at the Local," Alex laughed. "Lift off please Ronald."

At that, the two men gripped my upper arms tighter yet with two hands each now and hauled me up and a few good inches off the floor.

"HEY! Put me down you scum buckets!" I ranted as the two men swung my legs forward a few times... until two of the skin-headed patrons I had seen earlier at the pool table caught them by my combat booted feet. "FUCKERS, what is this shit?"

One of the skinheads was a mangy looking white guy and the other was a muscle bound taller than almost six feet black thug looking type.

"Go for it dudes, de-boot, de-pant and de-briefs this handsome soldier boy," Alex cackled as I was held aloft by the four men by my arms and legs.

Then, the two skinheads began doing just what Alex had said to do. They each began undoing the thick laces of my combat boots, grinning lecherously as they did their work.

"NAW, NAW! STOP IT! Stop this now!" I roared, facing forward as my boots were then taken off my feet, revealing my thick beige colored army issued calf-length and very sweaty and musty scented socks. "AWWW you FUCKERS!"

As I was held aloft Alex and Ronald licked my cheeks and administered sloppy wet Bugs Bunny like smooches to them as well, while at the same time the two skinheads dropped my boots to the floor and hoisted my socked feet higher... and up against their noses and mouths... AWWW JEEZ LOUISE!

"BASTARDS, PERVERTS, all of you!" I went on shouting as Alex and Ronald continued licking and smooching my face while the two ratty looking skinheads sniffed and snuffed heartily at my smelly-socked tootsies.

"MMM, nice U.S. soldier boy foot stink," the white skinhead said, holding my right foot by the ankle and sniffing and even fucking licking at my socked toes.

"DE-FUCKING-GENERATES!" I squabbled beyond angrily, realizing too that as I was kissed, licked and feet and sock worshipped while hoisted we had an audience of sleazy patrons watching the sorry spectacle that I was unwittingly starring in.

And lo and fucking behold my salt and peppered colored haired suit from the bar, the guy who had fingered my nametag and offered me any drink in the house on the house was part of that audience observing my humiliations. No way was I going to get any help from that guy, FUCK. It's really true I suppose about karma buds, what goes around comes back the fuck around.

"His pants now boys, if you would be so kind," Alex said next to the two skinheads.

With no hesitation whatsoever the two skinheads, or skins as they are sometimes referred to, reached for my belt.

"NO, NO, oh God no!" I snarled at that point through clenched teeth, struggling like a madman to free myself from the men's grasps, but with my hands tied so damned tight behind me that was futile.

FUCK, the next thing I knew, as I was still being held aloft, I was being relieved of my fatigue pants AND, oh God, AND my army issued olive green boxer shorts as well.

"FUCKING BASTARDS, lowlifes from hell, stripping me to my damned bare essentials!" I yelled stupidly.

"Nah, just down to your cute army socks Soldier boy," Ronald laughed as he and Alex, after the two skinheads had let go of my legs, lugged me over to what they called the milking stall.

They set me down in front of the structure and it was at that moment, up close and personal to it, that I saw the reason for the name they had coined it with.

For all intents and purposes it looked like any other stall in a men's room... except that the door of it looked to be constructed of a much stronger and thicker wood than the rest of the stalls at the Local... AND... now I saw what the handsome executive in just his shoes and socks said about said about having been milked and fucked beyond reason... BECAUSE there was a circular shaped hole cut in the stall door.

The hole was at crotch level AND it was obviously just big enough for a guy to stick his cock (and his balls if he chose to) through. It *was* what was called in the sleazy world of kink, a glory hole.

I knew, from things I had heard from gay buddies of mine that THIS hole was indeed called a glory hole. But the way I had heard it explained, a glory hole was usually cut in the sidewall of a stall, *not* in the front door of the structure. Oh fuck me hard bud, but with that hole cut in the front door of the stall and all the rope I saw piled up on the floor next to the stall, I now understood what Mr. Greg Smith had just recently endured here...

... it was to be the same thing I was about to endure, SHIT, SHIT, SHIT!"

"Unt eento zee stall weeth Soldier boy Meecan..." Alex chirped gleefully, this time in a campy sounding German accent.

"NO! NO! OH YOU FUCKERS!" I roared and struggled to no avail as moments later I was standing helplessly with my chest pressed up against the now closed stall door... and the two men were quickly and oh so fucking efficiently tying, binding and knotting me tight to the damned edifice. "OH SHIT, stop this, stop this sick horseplay now you dick heads!"

And speaking of yelling about dick heads, as I was being tied to the stall door of the milking stall, someone outside the stall worked my semi-hard cock... AND my balls through the infamous glory hole... I wondered if it was one of the skinheads from the pool table area, or maybe my suited admirer from the front bar. OH fuck who it was, the point was *a guy* was handling my pride and joy out there and putting it on display through a perversion called a damned glory hole, a milking hole at that.

"AWWW nooo! Get your hands off my privates whoever you are out there!" I ranted as I felt Alex and Ronald's knots binding me tighter and tighter to the stall door.

"Man, when a muscular dude is tied tight like this it really shows off his strength and musculature," Alex commented as he ogled me from the side, and then gave my ass cheeks a hard pinch.

"OWWW! Not funny you bastards, this is not funny at all!" I went on, staring stupidly at only the blank door in front of me. "I demand that you untie me, allow and permit me to re-clothe myself properly and exit this establishment of ill repute!"

"HA, establishment of ill repute indeed," Alex chortled next to me, gripping a handful of my flesh of one ass cheek and jiggling it as he spoke, causing me erotic pain and at the same time making my cock and balls outside the stall twitch a bit. "Which decade did you just parachute out of huh? That terminology went out way before you were even a glimmer in your father's sperm, HA!"

"FUCK YOU and the horse you rode in on you kidnapper, because when you really come down to it, that's what you hoods and scoundrels have done here at your establishment of ill repute, kidnapped a United States soldier, and that Sir, is truly a capital offense if ever I heard of one," I said, sounding somewhat country bumpkin even to myself, JEEZ, it had to be the humiliation and anger I was feeling at that moment.

But then, my words of admonishment were suddenly cut short and I gasped and grunted like a real soldier boy... because outside the stall, some skeevy perv had hunkered down at my on display private parts... and whoever he was, he had slurped my manhood into his mangy and greedy mouth...

"AWWWHHH, oh my fucking fucks, someone out there is sucking my damned baby maker," I seethed at Alex, he still standing next to me in my now stall prison, him and Ronald having finished binding me up to the damned stall door. "Fucking perverts, I did not come here for this..."

"No? Where do you usually go for it Soldier boy?" the guy who was sucking me asked me, holding my engorging cock in his hand and then quickly slurped me back into his damned craw.

"HA," I blurted loudly. "HA, ha, ha for you bud, very funny you are out there, trust me on this though, if I weren't all tied up like you mugs got me here you WOULD NOT be chowing on and feasting on my glorious cock out there!"

"All the more reason to have tied you up Soldier boy," Alex giggled next to me, reached into his pocket, brought out a long black silk cloth and quickly tied it over my eyes, effectively blindfolding me. "There you go Soldier, no need at this point for you to see anything."

"Bastard, bad enough you dimwits clobbered and captured me, stripped me and made me drink other men's piss and tied me the fuck up real tight and unforgiving like, *but now* you have to blindfold me as well?" I ranted and to my dismay and further humiliation, outside the stall, as the guy, whoever the fuck he was sucked me harder and harder I could feel my sperm offering boiling up in my nuts. "DAMN... "AWWWHHH fucking fucks, going to get my nut whoever you are out there Mr. Sucking My Cock, can't think of anything else to call you at this point... YUHHH..."

And with that, I did just that, shot a load big enough to choke a damned horse...

Standing beside me as I shot my load and shot my load right down the guy's throat outside the stall, Alex gave one of my big tits a squeeze and twist, which made me shoot my damned load even more... DANG, for a guy I really have sensitive titties I gotta say.

"UHHH... fucking titty monger you are as well huh bud?" I seethed, facing forward in damned blindfolded darkness as on one end of the stall door I was breathlessly shooting a load of soldier boy slop down some pervert's throat... and on the other side of the door one of the men who had so cleverly shanghaied me played with one of my big soldier-sized tits... HUMILIATING buds...

I went on grunting and groaning in a man's passion as I could detect that the guy outside the stall chowing down on my good stuff had arched his head back and was drinking from my font as if it was a fountain, GAWWWD buds... He tickled my dangling testicles a bit and lo and fucking behold, just like with my tit being worked, *that* caused me to jettison more of my soldier slop for the cum hungry bastard.

"AWWWHHH, f-feels like it won't ever stop," I whimpered in the forced ecstasy.

Suddenly, and as I had said that I felt it would never stop, I felt Alex, who was still standing mockingly next to me in the stall, pry my ass cheeks apart... and, OH NO, oh my fucks indeed buds, he started inching his pre-seeding hard cock into my rectal opening.

"H-HEYYY, NO, NO, tying me up like this and having me feasted on like a buffet at a wedding is one thing, but diddling and entering my backdoor is a horse of a whole other color you pervert!" I bantered, but to no avail...

... because as I shot the last of my first load of what would come to be one of the most humiliating nights of my life Alex speared me hard with his erection, stretching my ass walls... and fuck, fuck, fuck, I shot a hefty last blast of my cum... right down the greedy cock sucker's throat outside the stall...

"EEERRRHHH GAWWWD, someone do something here, this fucking perv in here with me is fucking my damned shit chute, OOO, shouldn't happen to a soldier boy of my level, bastards you all are," I panted as Alex rocked his cock in and out and in and out of my poor now de-virginized backdoor.

"HEE, HEE, HEE for you Soldier boy, because I guarantee this, I will not be the only dude fucking this sweet hole of yours in here tonight," Alex chortled from behind me, wrapped a hand around my neck, yanked my head back and kissed me a wet Bugs Bunny style kiss on the cheek, as he buried his cock in me till his balls were crashing against my ass cheeks.

As Alex kissed my cheek again my cock slipped out of the guy's mouth outside the stall, and before my poor exhausted manhood had a chance to deflate even a bit some other cock hungry degenerate gobbled it into his mouth... and began sucking me anew...

"AWWWHHH NO, no, AW man, don't be sucking me so soon after I've cum, oh my God, I'm all sensitive and sexy feeling in the cock right now you lowlife cock sucker out there," I prattled stupidly as I was cock sucked a second time and being ass fucked at the same goddamned time, *what a predicament.*

"I'll say yer sexy, Soldier boy," Alex laughed, fucked me harder and kissed my cheek again and again. "UHHH, yeah, could fuck you all night Soldier boy..."

And I had the horrid feeling that he meant it at that...

Outside the stall, as the second guy sucked my crank and as chills sped through me at what felt like hundreds of miles per hour I felt him toying with my army issued socks, rolling them up and down my calves as he sucked my cock like it was the holy grail of life...

"Fuck, bad enough he's a freak for sucking my cock, now he's playing with my damned army socks," I railed through clenched teeth, the pain in my hole monumental feeling at that point as Alex went on and fucking the tar out of me...

... but my soldier-sized cock didn't shrink once through the agony... and ecstasy? NO WAY!

After the guy outside the stall managed to suck a second load out of me, swallowing it all, just as his bud before him had done, and after Alex had pumped his load into me from behind, slapping my ass cheeks hard as he did so, I was given a few minutes of reprieve in that damned stall. I heard Alex climb out of the stall, leaving me there tied and blindfolded in just my damned army socks, my cock sticking out of the glory hole for anyone who wanted to suck it next... and me feeling totally humiliated and violated. As I stood there tied tight and in darkness I felt Alex's cum dripping out of my hole, GAWWWD... And tied to the door the way I was there was NO FUCKING WAY to pull my poor cock and balls into the stall, away from the sleazy cocksuckers and ball lickers out there in the men's room… FUCK, I was the feast for the night at the Local it seemed like…

A few minutes passed as I stood there catching my breath, sweating in my socks as it's come to be called and tears of rage and humiliation filled my eyes behind my damned blindfold… The need to piss again was setting in. Like a lot of dudes out there after I've cum I have to piss like a madman, and fuck me hard buds, (literally) I had cummed twice at that.

"HEY! HEY!" I roared to whoever might be outside the stall at that moment. "YO! I need to take a leak here! Could someone un-fucking-tie me so I can do so?"

From outside my stall prison I heard the sound of snickering and then Ronald's voice saying, "I'll help you out there Soldier boy, but you sure as hell aren't getting untied, at least not for a long while that is…"

Before I could respond to the fucker I felt his lips smooch themselves around just the tip of my spent cock.

"ARRRHHH, what in all fucks…" I muttered.

But then, when Ronald teased my cock slit with his tongue tip I knew what he intended. *He* was going to be my human urinal, JEEZ… Why in all hell did I make it known that I had to piss? Fucking Ronald grabbed my socked calves, squeezed them tight and diddled his tongue tip some more over my cock slit… *and* that's all it took to get me pissing good and heavy once more that night, that fateful night of nights…

"AWWW, fucker you are out there, scoffing down my soldier piss," I gurgled as Ronald sipped my piss from my slit as if it were a straw… and I have to admit the feeling of it as he drank my frothy lemonade made my blindfolded head spin all the more. "AWWWHHH… fucking fucks, the way you're drinking from my cock slit is somehow making my tits tingle in here…"

At that comment I heard the men who were gathered outside the stall all laugh raucously, meanly and mockingly…

Once Ronald was done doing the nasty of drinking my piss offering I heard him say that he had to get back to work at the bar with Alex and he left the damned men's room... and not five minutes later, another guy had my poor numb feeling cock in his mouth... and he was sucking me up to a new but this time, *painful* erection...

I leaned my forehead against the stall door and cried miserably under my blindfold...

After the guy, whoever the fucking fuck he was, managed to siphon another load out of me, getting me screaming and guttering in a mixture of agony and twisted ecstasy I suddenly felt the presence of someone standing next to me in the damned stall. Obviously someone had climbed in there with me.

"WH-who's there?" I croaked, as the last droplets of my cum dripped from my overly sucked cock outside the stall.

"You can call me Mr. Barber Soldier boy," I heard someone say from behind me, and then, suddenly, I heard the sound of a battery operated clipper whir to life.

"HEY, WHAT THE FUCK MAN?" I ballyhooed as the guy began using his electric clipper to shear away my hair. "I'm a damned Staff Sergeant, I don't need to be head-shaved down to peach fuzz, *fucking bastard!*"

But my pleas and demands went on deaf ears as the guy ran his clippers over and over my head, shearing away my piss scented hair, seeing as it had been piss soaked earlier, inching his way around my blindfold in the process.

"AW yeah, gets me all worked up when I shave a dude's head, even more-so if the dude is a handsome soldier boy like you are," the guy tittered as he did his damned dirty work of shaving my head, which I would find would be the prelude to what he planned for me.

"So glad you're having the time of your life here bud," I said sarcastically.

But let's face it, I really wasn't in a position for being catty and venomous, I was the one all stripped, tied and blindfolded after all. Once the guy was done shearing away all my hair he turned off his electric clipper and then I felt it, oh my fucks, I felt it. The guy grabbed my ass cheeks, pried them apart and began inserting his steely feeling erection into me...

"AWWWHHH, fuck, you weren't kidding huh Mr. Sick Barber?" I railed through clenched teeth. "Shaving a soldier boy's head really does get you all worked up huh? *Especially in the cock...*"

"Yeah, and it's not every time I shave a dude's head that I get to bury myself in him afterwards," the barber guy said, pressed his lips against the back of my neck and kissed me there over and over as he proceeded to fuck the tar out of me... the second fucking my ass would get that night, GAWWWDDD...

Once more, as I was fucked in the ass in the stall, as the barber pounded his way in and out of me, outside the stall my numb cock twitched and danced stupidly in the wind.

Then, with his lips pressed against the back of my neck and his hard cock buried deep inside me and stretching my ass walls to what felt like epic proportions the barber shot his load... and oh so deep inside me, cumming like a banshee it felt like. I could feel his thick warm fluids sluicing in my innards.

"PERVERT, fucking sleazy scumbag you are," I whimpered as he pressed up hard against my back, kissing my neck and slobbering on me as he seemed to cum and cum.

As he grunted and groaned in a man's passion I cried miserably behind the damned blindfold and wondered how I was ever going to get out of this godforsaken mess, and how I would deal with it later on at that...

When the barber guy was done cumming his cum inside me he snickered meanly as his cock deflated and slowly slid out from inside me. What a horrid feeling that was, let me tell you buds...

And then, as soon as he was there he was gone, and even though I was blindfolded I could just picture all my hair all over the stall floor... DAMN it all...

Again I stood there trapped and helpless, catching my breath... How would I get out of this was what kept running through my mind... I knew for a fact that the twisted bar owners were not going to release me any time soon. I'm sure they wanted more of their cock hungry patrons to suck me off some more... and God only knew how many more guys would choose to ram my ass fuck-wise...

For a while the bathroom was silent, the only noise I heard was coming from the bar, outside the bathroom. I tried a few times, most unsuccessfully I might add, to get my hands untied. FUCK, those bastards had tied me too tight... I stupidly thought how Alex and Ronald must have been boy scouts to have learned to tie knots so damned tight, HAR, HAR, but sadly this joke tonight was totally on me buds...

But then, as I stood there tottering stupidly on my socked tootsies I heard the men's room door open and then close, and then, at first I thought my ears were deceiving me... because I heard the sounds of women's high-heeled shoes approaching the stall, *the milking stall... and in my case, literally, the fucking stall.* As I thought that my cum slopped asshole twitched, JEEZ.

"H-hey, who's out there?" I cautiously called out, wondering why women would be in the men's room, no, fuck that, I wondered why any women would be at the Local itself.

"Oh my goodness gracious, just look at the size of that, now that is delicatessen quality pepperoni if I ever saw one," I heard a lisping but deep voice saying and then a slender but firm hand was gripping my semi hardness outside the stall.

FUCK, the women who had come into the men's room weren't really women at all, they were drag queens, men dressed as women, even blindfolded I knew that, FUCCCKKK!

And drag was just another fetish obviously embraced at the sleazy establishment called the Local... As the drag queen handled what she had called my delicatessen quality pepperoni sized cock I felt her long claw-like fingernails trailing along the shaft of it, getting some breathless soldier sounding grunts out of me.

As the first drag queen handled my cock I felt fingertips caressing and stroking my testicles.

"Hey you ladies out there, please, please be gentle with my pride and joy huh?" I called out, grinning stupidly behind my damned blindfold. "They uh, they haven't had an easy time of it tonight.

The two drag queens giggled like mean school girls and then, after they had stroked me up to a new and pain-filled erection and managed to get my poor balls hanging even lower than normal I felt a something that felt real snug and tight snapped onto the base of my manhood.

"AWWWHHH, what in all fucks?" I babbled, struggling mightily now against the ropes binding me to the stall door.

"That will keep you nice and stacked up in the cock for the next time you cum tonight Soldier boy in the stall," one of the drag queens laughed and teased my piss slit with the tip of one of her what felt like razor-sharp fingernails.

"Nice way to refer to me bitch, I can honestly say that you two are no ladies, not by a long shot," I garbled madly. "What have you two done to my poor over-used cock out there huh?"

"Just cock-ringed you Soldier boy in the stall," the other drag queen replied and snaked her fingernails over my testicles again, teasing the bejesus out of them, making my erection twitch like a thing alive. "And like Samantha here just said, that will keep you real stacked up the next time you cum tonight…"

"FUCCCKKK, what sick torture is this?" I ranted. "You mean that the next pervert who sucks me off and gets my nut, being cock-ringed like you two bitches from hell have me now I won't be able to go soft? SHIT, *that* is diabolical…

As I reeled my tirade the two drag queens giggled more and more…

Seconds later, the two drag queens had climbed into the stall with me… and were standing at my sides, no doubt in their gigantic high heels. To have climbed into the stall in their high heels they had to be real nimble I stupidly thought.

"Oh my, he is a handsome soldier boy," the drag queen on my left commented shrilly and mockingly, trailing her hand and fingernails over my newly bald head.

"Bitches, how about doing the right thing and untying me and taking this damned blindfold off me as well?" I demanded, facing forward as the two drag queens were then trailing their slender palms and fingernails over my ass cheeks, squeezing them, kneading them, jiggling them.

As they worked their black magic on my melon-shaped well-muscled ass cheeks I felt my cock outside the stall tingling like crazy. Fuck me hard buds, but was this possible? After all the cums I had cummed that night was it possible I could cum again? And from what the two drag queens were doing to my damned ass cheeks at that?

But then, oh God, THEN, my thought process was cut short, as I felt my sexy ass cheeks once more being pried apart, revealing my cum sopped bunghole...

"AWWW NO, NO, not this again you bitches," I pleaded miserably.

The two drag queens took turns plowing and thrusting in and out of me, fucking my poor hole anew.

"FFFUUUCCCKKK, I can honestly say, you two are *no* ladies," I hemmed and the two drag queens laughed meanly, squeezing the tar out of my ass cheeks as they fucked me six ways from Sunday it felt like. "BITCHES, diddling my diddler..."

DAMN, for men who dressed like women they sure had big cocks, and that's no joke buds...

When they shot their loads inside me, like the dudes before them had done they kissed me hard and left lipstick smears on the back of my big bull-sized neck and bald head, panting and shrilling like two women as they cummed and cummed...

One of them wrapped her arms around me, grabbed my nipples with her claw-like fingers and squeezed the tar out of them, as she cummed and cummed and cummed... and as she did so, outside the stall, OH MY GOD, another cock hungry bar patron slurped my now cock-ringed manhood into his mouth... and began sucking me in earnest...

"AWWW, bastard out there, and bitches from hell in here, getting it from both ends this time," I squabbled crazily and my eyes crossed in my head under my damned blindfold. "FFFUUUCCCKKK..."

As whoever it was outside the stall sucking my cock sucked me harder and harder, determined it seemed to get that pain-filled load from my cock-ringed manhood, he tugged meanly and PAINFULLY on my poor testicles at the same time...

"RRRHHH... what a night this turned out to be for me! GAWWD!" I screeched then as I felt my balls giving up what would definitely be their last load for the night.

As I shot my load down the guy's gullet outside the stall the second drag queen finished shooting her load into me rectal-wise, squeezing and smacking my ass cheeks at the same time.

"HUUUHHH shooting my load and shooting my load and shooting my load and being filled with load at the same time," I grunted like a nut, my head spinning like crazy now. "AND FUCK, my cock is still so hard out there... what a twisted turn of events all this is..."

The two drag queens laughed like the mean bitches they were, kissed me goodbye and then I heard them climbing out of the stall, leaving me alone in there once more, and my poor hole aching all the more as well... JEEZ... and not to mention that my cock and balls were aching on the other side of the stall as well, hard as steel and hanging REAL low, even though I had just shot ANOTHER load for some pervert who was hungry for soldier boy spunk...

Once more the men's room was quiet...

I pressed my forehead against the stall door and whimpered miserably, waiting for a second wind of strength so that I could try again to get myself loose... *and* out of that godforsaken stall at the equally godforsaken bar called the Local...

After a good five minutes or so had passed I took a deep breath and started struggling like a madman against the ropes fastening me to the damned stall door. Every time my cock twitched and swung outside the stall door it ached miserably. I HAD TO get that cock ring off it buds...

But all my struggles against the ropes were to no avail, I was tied too damned tight, and being blindfolded made it all the more difficult. I cried tears of rage behind the damned blindfold.

But then, suddenly, I found my luck changing, because from outside the stall I could feel the ropes binding me to the stall door being undone... and, oh thank God, and the cock ring was taken off my manhood as well. My cock started to deflate to normal proportions. Granted, it would be a while before I would lay another erection but at least that damned monstrosity was off it.

"Hey, who's that?" I called out. "Thanks man, thanks, untie me, fucking untie me..."

"No problem Soldier boy McCann..." I heard a familiar sounding voice say to me as the ropes started falling away. "Bad enough they did this to *me* countless times. I won't stand by and watch it done to a fellow serviceman..."

Fuck me hard, it was that handsome executive, the guy who had been tied up in the stall before me, Greg Smith.

When all the ropes that had been tethering me to the stall door fell away I took a few steps back so Mr. Smith could push the stall door open and get my hands untied for me.

As I felt my cock and balls slide through and out of the glory hole a wave of relief swept through me. I heard the stall door pushed open and a second later the blindfold was whipped off me. I stood there in just my socks staring upwards into Mr. Greg Smith's beautiful dark eyes.

"Thank you Sir can't say how much I appreciate what you just did for me," I said as the handsome executive stepped behind me and untied my hands.

"A joke is one thing, but taking it to these levels is another," Greg Smith said and once my hands were untied and as I was massaging my wrists I looked outside the stall and saw that my fatigue pants and my boots were piled up on a sink. Just like Mr. Greg Smith it looked like someone had stolen my damned underpants. No matter, I was out of the stall and soon I would be out of the damned Local.

"I couldn't agree more Sir," I said. "What those fuckers did to me shouldn't happen to any serviceman."

A short while later, fully dressed, I was back in my car, the need to piss finally relieved in more ways than one, I drove toward Fort Kensington... and as I drove my soft cock tingled in my fatigue pants...... and in my pants pocket were Mr. Greg Smith's black socks, a souvenir from him as a way to never forget him and what we had both shared at the sleazy establishment of ill repute, "The Local…"

The End

Thinking of Greg Smith… wherever he may be…

Tickling Arthur's Feet

A Male Tickle Fetish Story

Author: Originally written as: Christopher Rosalie, and now: Christopher Trevor

My wife and I were going to buy a house. I could not believe it. After being married for three years and paying rent to a landlord we could not stand, we were able to afford a house. All of our scrimping and saving had finally paid off. I was at work when I received the call from a Real Estate Agency that we had been dealing with that they wanted to show us a choice house as soon as possible.

It was nine thirty AM on the dot when my office phone rang.

"Chase Bank, Arthur Gimble speaking," I said politely into the receiver. "How can I help you?"

"Good morning Mr. Gimble, this is Alex from Good Time Realty, how are you this morning Sir?" one of the real estate agents that my wife and I had been dealing with asked in greeting.

"Fine Alex, good to hear from you," I replied, leaning back in my chair and crossing my wingtip shoed feet in front of me under my desk. "Do you have some good news for me this morning?"

"Actually I do Mr. Gimble," Alex said enthusiastically. "There's a beautiful two bedroom duplex house available that I would love to show you and your wife. It went on the market last night and I doubt it'll last long. That's why I'm calling you so early."

"Sounds nice," I said. "Is it in an area we discussed?"

"Right in the heart of it Sir," Alex responded. "Now, if possible I can show it to you in an hour. Do you think you and your wife could take the morning off to come and see it?"

"Oh shit, my wife is in a business meeting all morning today," I said, sounding disappointed.

"That's too bad Mr. Gimble," Alex said, sounding equally as disappointed as I. "How does your schedule look?"

"Fuck man, I haven't taken a day off in the last two years," I said with a grin. "I think this bank is out for my blood, Alex."

We both laughed politely at my snide remark.

"Heh, the wonderful world of banking, eh Mr. Gimble?" Alex asked me. "Do you think you could take some time off today to see the house?"

"Yeah, sure, I can take the morning off," I said enthusiastically. "Fuck that, I can take the entire day off. Where is the house?"

As Alex recited the address of the house in the Dyker Heights area of Brooklyn, New York I quickly jotted it down on a piece of paper.

"Okay Alex, just let me call my wife's office and leave a message there so she knows what I'm up to," I said. "I'll clear this with my vice president and be on my way. I should see you there in an hour and a half."

"Good deal Mr. Gimble," Alex said.

"Thanks man," I said happily and we hung up.

I picked up the phone and called my wife's office number. Her secretary answered on the second ring.

"Mrs. Gimble's office," the young man named Dave said politely.

"Hi Dave, its Arthur," I said.

"Good morning Mr. Gimble, how are you today?" Dave asked me respectfully.

"I'm fine Dave, you?" I asked in response.

"Just fine Sir," Dave said. "Mrs. Gimble is in a meeting and…"

"I know Dave; I know she'll probably be in that meeting all morning," I said, finishing the secretary's sentence for him. "Could you please tell her that I received a call from Good Time Realty and that I'm going to check out a house for us in Dyker Heights?"

"Sure will Mr. Gimble," Dave said happily. "Congratulations."

"Thanks Dave, but we haven't gotten the house yet," I went on. "Please tell my wife that I'm taking the rest of the day off and I'll call her when I get home."

"Yes Sir, Mr. Gimble," Dave said.

"Take care Dave, talk to you soon," I said before hanging up.

"Good-bye Mr. Gimble, have a good day and good luck," Dave gushed and we both hung up.

I always had a feeling that Dave had some sort of crush on me. The few times I had met him when I went to my wife's office to pick her up before we went out to dinner on Friday nights once in a while I couldn't help but notice the way he looked at me. It really didn't bother me though. I mean, when I was in college I was the captain of the football team and there were a few gay guys who had crushes on me. I mean, admittedly it gave me a boner to know that someone was getting aroused by me, but it was when the girls had crushes on me that I really boned up. But hey, so what if guys had crushes on me? I'm a handsome dude after all... and to each his own, right?

I stood up, grabbed my suit jacket off the back of my chair, stuffed the paper with the house address written on it into my pocket and dashed out of my office. I told my vice president that I was going to need a personal day. When Mr. Jacob heard why I would need the rest of the day off he gave me a hard clap on the back, a wish for good luck and told me to be on my way... I walked out of the office building a little while later, practically on winged feet. HA, I had no idea at that moment just how much my poor feet would suffer that day... that fateful day...

My name is Arthur Gimble. I'm thirty years old, an executive with Chase bank. I have short cut brown hair, parted on the side in a banker's fashion and chestnut shaped eyes. I'm five feet nine inches tall. I started out at Chase bank as a teller when I was nineteen years old and going to college at nights studying business law. Through a lot of hard work, four years of college and two years of banking school I worked my way up the corporate ladder. At the age of thirty I was in charge of the Customer Account department and also in charge of a few of the bank's key accounts as well. Three years ago I married the girl of my dreams. And now we were prepared to buy a house.

Yes, it sure seemed that everything was falling into place in my life. I didn't know as I headed for the subway to Brooklyn that I would myself would fall into place that day, actually I would fall stupidly and helplessly into place while checking out the house in Dyker Heights.

Dressed in a navy blue pinstriped suit, white shirt, a dark red silk necktie and black lace-up wingtips I dashed down the steps to the subway station...

I arrived in Dyker Heights a little more than an hour later. The walk from the subway station to the house that Alex had called about was ten minutes. Not bad I thought. The neighborhood was excellent with plenty of stores within walking distance. When I reached the house I was awe struck at the sight of it. It was perfect, exactly what my wife and I were looking for. Well, from the outside it looked like what we were looking for. It was two stories tall, red brick faced and had new insulated windows.

As I stood there with my hands tucked in my suit pants pockets staring at the house the front door opened and a tall, rugged looking guy in bone colored khakis, a light blue button down shirt opened at the collar and brown suede wingtips came walking out. He had dark brown wavy hair and very dark brown eyes. He actually had the build and the look of a boxer. He was slightly taller than me.

"Mr. Gimble?" the man asked me as he approached, a huge hand outstretched for me to shake.

"Uh, yes," I said and took his hand to shake.

"I'm Ronald, Alex's associate," Ronald said, pumping my hand hard, squeezing it tight. "Alex asked me to tell you that he couldn't make it, that he got sort of tied up. So he asked me to show you the house, if you don't mind that is."

"No, not at all, it's nice to meet you Ronald," I said as the guy continued holding tight to my hand.

"Same here Mr. Gimble, well, shall we go see what there is to see?" Ronald said happily.

He let go of my hand (finally) and I cheerily told him to lead the way. We walked together into the house.

"Alex tells me that you and your wife will be first time home owners," Ronald said, making light conversation.

"Yeah, that's true," I replied, looking around as we walked in.

The main floor was very spacious. The entrance led into a large living room, which connected to the dining room and kitchen. We walked slowly side by side as I took it all in.

"Obviously this is the living room," Ronald said.

"Very nice," I said softly, already picturing what it would look like once me and my wife had it furnished. "Very nice indeed."

We walked through the dining room and to the kitchen. The place was clean as a whistle and smelled fresh.

"The basement is through that door," Ronald said, pointing to a door at the far end of the kitchen.

"Basement?" I asked him. "Alex said this was a duplex, but he didn't mention it had a basement."

"Would you like to see it?" Ronald asked me, taking me by the arm and walking me toward the door.

"Sure thing, this great, a fucking basement too," I said happily, not believing our luck.

Ronald let go of my arm, opened the basement door, clicked on the light and I followed him down the steps, into hell.

"Wow, with a basement we'll have plenty of extra room for storage," I said.

"Yeah, and not to mention a playroom for your kids," Ronald said as we descended the steps.

"Well, my wife and I don't have kids, at least not yet," I said and slid out of my suit jacket, draping it over my arm.

When Ronald and I reached the bottom of the steps I looked around the large barren room, well, barren except for a strange looking device that was placed right in the very center of the room. The basement was clean. It looked like it had recently been completely done over. As we moved further into the large room my eyes were riveted to the weird looking device that I just mentioned.

"What is that thing?" I asked curiously as we approached it.

It was two wooden straight back chairs facing each other. On the back of one chair dangled a pair of handcuffs. On the chair facing it was what looked like a pair of wooden stocks, right out of the seventeen hundreds, along with a pair of c-clamps holding the stocks to the chair. On a small table in front of the second chair was an old-fashioned record player. Hooked up to the turntable, which was tilted at just about sixty degrees, was a pair of wooden sticks attached to the spindle in the center... and on the ends of the sticks I saw feathers.

"Say, what is this thing?" I asked, crouching down next to the chair with the stocks on it and running the palm of my hand over them.

"It's the last thing the previous owner of the house has to come and take," Ronald replied. "I think it used to be upstairs. He told me that he used it for parties."

"I don't understand," I said. "What does it do?"

Asking that question was the worst thing I could have done. My inquisitive nature was about to land me into the strangest situation and predicament I would ever find myself in to date.

"Well, it's really difficult to explain Mr. Gimble," Ronald responded, looking at the device with a hand cupped under his chin. "Here, put your suit jacket on the back of this chair, have a seat, stretch your legs out and I'll attempt to show you."

"Okay," I said.

I draped my suit jacket over the chair with the handcuffs dangling on the back of it and sat down.

"Okay, now I think that the way it works is that your feet go into the stocks," Ronald said and without even asking wrapped a strong hand around one of my navy blue socked ankles.

He lifted my foot, stretching out my leg, opened the stocks and placed my foot in it, at the ankle.

"You can place your other foot in this one," Ronald said, pointing to the other opening in the stocks.

I stupidly did as he said. Then, with my feet encased in the stocks Ronald pushed them closed, using the hinges on the sides to secure them shut.

"It's used as a way to enhance parties," Ronald went on explaining and crouched down next to the chair I was seated in.

Without any hesitation he gently pulled my hands behind me toward the open handcuffs.

"Hey, what are you doing?" I asked sounding and feeling very nervous all of a sudden.

"Well Mr. Gimble, in order for you to get the full effect of this thing you need to be fully encased in it," Ronald said and quickly locked one of the handcuffs around my wrist.

The metal was cold and before I could utter a word Ronald quickly locked my other wrist in the other handcuff.

"Okay, now if this record player works you'll get the full effect of this thing for sure Mr. Gimble," Ronald said, getting to his feet.

So there I was, handcuffed to a chair with my damned feet locked in a pair of stocks. I nervously wriggled my fingers and my socked toes. I watched as Ronald switched on the record player and the turntable began spinning the sticks with the feathers on the ends of them around and around. On the turntable speed of 45 RPMs, it was moving pretty fast. I watched as the feathers on the ends of the sticks spun around and moved all over the bottoms of my (still) shoed and socked feet.

"See?" Ronald asked me, looking down sort of hungrily at my feet (what was up with that?) "It's called an Executive Tickle Torture machine."

"Yeah, so I see," I said, my heart pounding wildly.

Ronald again cupped his chin in his hand and seemed to mull the situation over.

"This isn't right," he said. "You're still not getting the full effect."

With that said he turned off the record player.

"WH-what do you mean?" I asked him as he began unlacing my wingtips. "H-hey, what are you doing?"

"In order for you to really understand this thing you need to have your shoes and socks off Mr. Gimble," Ronald explained, his fingers working quickly in getting my shoelaces undone.

"H-HEY, don't, don't take my shoes off me man," I stammered in fear now, realizing all too late what all I was in for.

Executive Tickle Torture machine? Oh fuck, EXECUTIVE TICKLE TORTURE MACHINE? The words suddenly took on a horrible meaning for me. Fuck man, I was an executive and I was trapped in that fucking thing! OH GOD! Slowly, Ronald slid my spit-polished wingtips from my feet. Or should I say my size ten extremely ticklish feet?

"Ronald no, no man, don't DO NOT take my shoes off me!" I pleaded.

"But Mr. Gimble, I want you to really enjoy this machine," Ronald said and I nearly blanched when I saw him sniff the insides of my shoes.

A look of ecstasy came over the guy's face and he sniffed heartily again at the insides of my shoes, his tongue hanging out of his mouth. Then, I watched as he slobbered and sucked and licked at the insides of my shoes.

"Fuck man and holy shit, what is going on here?" I asked desperately. "What are you licking my damned shoes for?"

Without replying Ronald placed my shoes on the floor and then crouched down in front of my blue nylon ribbed socked feet. To my utter disbelief, he ran his tongue slowly and methodically over and over the bottoms of my feet, sending chills through me.

"OH MY GOD, you pervert, you fucking pervert, licking my damned smelly socked feet," I seethed. "Ronald, let me out of this thing. I swear, I'll tell Alex about this and you will lose your job."

"I don't work for Alex," Ronald said softly and sucked my big toes, holding my feet tightly in his big hands.

"Y-you don't work for Alex?" I asked in incredulity. "B-but you said you were his associate."

"I lied Mr. Gimble, I lied," the guy said with a sneer, sounding almost like Paul Lynde, looking up at me now as he held my feet tightly, his thumbs pressed hard against the bottoms of them. "I'm actually the owner of this house. This device is my invention. The day you and your wife were in Alex's office I was there. I took an instant shine to you.

You sitting there all decked out in your business suit, your wingtips, your silk tie and these executive socks I truly adore, it was overwhelming for me Mr. Gimble."

As he spoke he gave the bottom of one of my feet a long slathering lick, sending more chills through me as he pressed his tongue hard against the meaty bottom of my foot.

"You see, I have this fetish for tickle torturing handsome executive's feet," Ronald said, let go of my feet and stood up. "And you fit the bill perfectly Mr. Gimble."

"T-tickle my feet?" I asked and gulped hard, knowing, knowing oh so well just how tickle sensitive the bottoms of my feet really are.

"Yep, and as luck would have it I was in the office today when Alex called you to come here and see the house," Ronald said, the tips of his fingers starting to work at the toes of my socks, slowly taking them off me. "I told him I had to get a few last minute things out of the house and that I would show you around, giving him time to finish up some work in the office."

I was starting to sweat as Ronald slowly slid my damned socks off my feet through the stocks.

"OH GOD, Ronald, no, d-don't take my socks off me man!" I begged, knowing full well at that point what I was in for. "Oh shit you fucker!"

When my feet were bare Ronald balled my socks up in his hand and placed his fingers on the switch on the record player. My eyes opened wide in outright terror.

"Now you'll get the full effect of my invention Mr. Gimble," Ronald said happily.

NO, no, don't turn it on man!" I pleaded desperately.

With a wicked looking grin on his face Ronald switched the record player on and set the speed control of the turntable at 78

RPMs. The two sticks were set in rapid spinning motion and the feathers at the ends of them were instantly tickling the bottoms of my bare feet.

"OOOHHH, HA, HA, HA!" I was suddenly guffawing helplessly. "OH SHIT, OH SHIT, OH FUCKING SHHHIIITTT, tur-turn it off man, PL-PLEASE, Ronald, turn it the fuck off! HA, HA, Ha, ha, ha, oh my Lord in Heaven, I'm being tickle tortured here!"

Smiling down at me Ronald bounced my balled up socks up and down in his hands a few times, sniffed them heartily and then stuffed them in his pants pocket.

"I'll be keeping these great scented socks of yours as a souvenir of this little conquest Mr. Gimble," Ronald said merrily as I sat there laughing uncontrollably. "Actually, I would hardly even call this a conquest. It was beyond simple to get you into that thing. When you get out is a whole other story."

"Y-you fucker, HA, HA, HA, HA! Y-you can have my damned stinking socks! I have plenty of back-up pairs!" I seethed. "JUST pl-please, turn this wretched thing off! OHHH GOD, ha, ha, ha!"

But instead Ronald secured the c-clamps on the outside of the stocks around the bottoms of my toes, forcing my poor feet to remain perfectly still as they were tickle tortured.

"HO, HO, HO, ha, ha, ha, th-this is sick man!" I screamed in a high-pitched tone of voice.

"When I saw you with that pretty wife of yours at Alex's office I just knew that you would be a good candidate for my executive tickle torture machine Mr. Gimble!" Ronald said, squatting down next to me and loosening my tie and unbuttoning the top button of my shirt. "Young, strong minded executive like you is the perfect type of guy for this invention of mine."

"F-FUCKER, HA, HA, HA, HAAA!" I gasped, looking up at the trickster as he tugged on my silk tie.

"Now, the way I see it, two hours of this should be a good warm-up for what I have planned," Ronald said, pulling my tie down even further, loosening the knot in it as he went.

"T-TWO hours? HA, HA, HA, HA!" I gasped in disbelief. "I-I'll laugh to death by then! OOOHHH GAWD, ha, ha, ha, FUCKING FUCKS, I-I can't take this man!"

"Sure you can Mr. Gimble, you're a lot stronger than you're giving yourself credit for," Ronald said and slid my tie off me. "You're a strong minded executive. A guy like you should be able to deal with more than a few hours of this."

"OOOHHH SH-SHIT, ha, ha, ha! YOU, you can't mean this!" I sputtered. "I-I have to be back at work soon."

"No you don't," Ronald said quickly. "I know from Alex that you took the entire day off to come and check this house out."

My little lie hadn't panned out, SHIT!

"See, see if, ha, ha, ha, ha! See if my wife and I will buy this place!" I spat angrily at the guy. "Y-you can't kidnap a potential buyer and tickle torture him like this! HA, HA, HA, HA!"

"Oh you'll buy it," Ronald said, unbuttoning my white starting to soak up with sweat dress shirt. "When you hear the price I'm asking you and your wife won't be able to resist it Mr. Gimble. And I am sure you will want me to keep the tickle torture device here. As a matter of fact, I can promise that you'll want me to come here and tickle torture you on a regular basis. You really were so easy to get into that device. And after this is over today you will be begging for it, mark my words."

"Y-you're out of your fucking mind, ha, ha, ha, ha!" I chortled crazily.

He got my shirt fully unbuttoned and spread the sides of it out, exposing my hairy cheat and big pink fleshy nipples.

"AH, just as I was hoping, nice big meaty tits," Ronald said and squeezed one of my nipples hard, rolling it around between his fingertips, sending even more chills through me.

"F-fucking pervert, leave my damned tits alone!" I laughed. "HA, ha, ha, OOOHHH, HO, HO, HO, HO…"

Looking at me sadistically now Ronald stood up, towering over me.

"After two hours, I'll give you a five minute break, and then we'll go for another hour of tickling those cute feet of yours," Ronald quipped.

"AF-after two hours of this I-I'll be beyond crazy man!" I gasped, knowing there was no way out at that point. "HA, ha, ha, ha!"

From his other pocket Ronald produced a pair of mean looking sharp-teethed tit clamps.

"Now these will make you crazy for sure," Ronald said, holding up the tit clamps.

If I hadn't been laughing so damned hard I would have broken down in tears for sure at that point. Ronald palmed the tit clamps, climbed over me and stood over my prone body and began rolling his fingertips tightly over my damned nipples, really, REALLY squeezing the fucking fuck out of them.

"HA, ha, ha, ha, ha! GODS, can't believe y-you've got me in this damned position man!" I garbled as Ronald's fingers really worked the fuck out of my nipples.

I agree to a point Mr. Gimble," Ronald said as he REALLY put the screws to twisting and kneading my nipples. "Although somehow I think that somewhere deep inside you, you wanted to be in this position, somehow I think tickling is more a part of you than you're admitting to here."

I was laughing too hard and feeling too much in the way of chills to reply to what Ronald had just said... true as it might have been at that...

It was a good fifteen minutes or so later when the fucking guy stopped working my nipples. I was a sweating mess of jelly by then let me tell you. Ronald tweaked my nipples up to two pointy masses of hard flesh on my chest. They stuck out nice and pointy, like two bullets.

"G-GOD no," I gasped as Ronald opened the hungry looking tit clamps and moved them toward the two numbed nubs that were my danged nipples.

Leaning down over me he clipped the tit clamps onto my poor nipples. They bit hard and cruelly into them.

"ARRRHHH, ha, ha, ha, ha!" I heaved miserably at that point, laughing and in erotic pain at the same time.

Ronald stepped back to the side of the chair I was trapped on and looked at me with a fiendish grin.

"I have lots of stuff in mind for you Mr. Gimble," Ronald said, glancing down at my being-tickled feet and then he looked back into my eyes as I laughed and cackled like a damned maniac. "By the time this day is over and I send you home to your wife to tell her the good news about your new home, you will be a changed man."

"WH-why me you bastard? HA, HA, HA, HA!" I cackled madly.

"Just a feeling I got when I saw you in the Real Estate office with your wife and Alex," Ronald responded. "When I saw you sitting there with those hot feet of yours wrapped around the sides of the chair you were seated on the sight of those sexy wingtips and your dark colored socks drove me wild. Somehow I knew that I had to get you here and in this position."

"HA, ha, ha, ha, ha!" I laughed loudly. "G-get me here indeed, s-sick fuck you are, ha, ha, ha, ha!"

"Although at first I never thought it would be as easy as it was getting you hooked up in that thing," he said. "I truly thought I was going to have to really do some storytelling to convince you to get in there."

Ronald reached down, pulled on the chain hanging between the tit clamps and a surge of pain mixed with ecstasy coursed through me at what felt like a hundred miles per hour. He pulled on the chain till my poor nipples felt as if they would be ripped clear off my chest. Despite the pain, I laughed and roared loudly. The fucking guy then let go of the chain and stepped behind me, placed his hands on my shoulders and squeezed them tightly.

"I have to go out for a while, but don't worry, I'll be back in time for your break when your first two hours of tickle time are up," Ronald said, leaning down and licked one of my earlobes as my head bobbed around from my laughter.

"G-going out?" I gasped. "HA, HA, HA, HA, HA! Y-you can't leave me here like this Ronald! I-I'll go stir crazy. HA, HA, HA, HA! OH MY GOD, my poor tits..."

"I want to go and tell Alex how much you liked the house and that you will indeed be buying it," Ronald said, letting go of my shoulders. "And not to worry Mr. Gimble, this basement is soundproof, so please laugh, roar and cackle all you want. I insist on it actually."

I was doing just that that was for sure. Then, to further my horrible situation even more, Ronald tied my silk necktie over my eyes, blindfolding me.

"OHHH GOD, you miserable bastard!" I ranted, as being blindfolded now made the tickling sensations and the pressure on my nipples worsen about a hundred times over. "HA, ha, ha, ha, ha! HOOO, hooo, hooo, this, this is too much man!"

But then, the sounds of Ronald's footsteps as he ascended the stairs out of the basement, oh God. When I heard the door to the basement open and then close my heart sank in despair.

"HA, ha, ha, ha!" I laughed miserably, heaving my muscular chest up and down in the chair.

Each time I moved my chest the pain in my nipples worsened. To my utter surprise and dismay I found that my big uncut sausage-sized cock was piss hard in my damned suit pants...

So there I was, stretched out between two chairs, handcuffed, my bared feet trapped in a pair of stocks, blindfolded, tit clamped and having my poor feet tickle tortured. Sweat broke out all over my exposed chest and dripped down to my stomach area. My feet started sweating as well of course as those blasted feathers spun and spun over them, doing their dirty work, I laughed and laughed, desperately trying to catch just one even breath in between my loud cackling. I wriggled my toes in misery and my cock pounded big and hard in my suit trousers. I frantically tried my best not to piss.

"HO, ho, ho, ho, ho, ho, ho, ha, ha, ha!" I roared then with my head tilted back, looking up at the unseen ceiling. "I-I'll fucking kill Ronald for this!"

Thoughts of my wife and I looking for a house and how it had led me to this blasted situation went through my tortured mind. Thoughts of my wife being in her business meeting and not having a clue as to what had happened to me went through my tortured mind. Thoughts of my wife handling my dirty socks from the laundry bag and complaining about how badly they smelled went through my tortured mind. Thoughts of Ronald slipping my smelly socks off my feet and sniffing them heartily went through my tortured mind. Thoughts of that bastard stealing my socks filled my tortured mind. Thoughts of how very stupid I had been to allow myself into this predicament engulfed my tortured mind.

"HA, ha, ha, ha, ha!" I roared miserably. "OH GOD!"

Saliva dribbled from my trembling lips and by then my body was bathed in sweat. My suit trousers were stuck to me, my BVD briefs were sweat sopped and my damned cock was aching, hard, and the need to piss was overwhelming by then. As I sat there with my head hanging down, laughing, laughing, laughing and laughing uncontrollably tears of rage formed behind my sweat soaked tie turned blindfold. After a while more I simply lost track of the time...

I was still laughing, screaming with it actually two hours later...

I heard the sound of the basement door opening and then Ronald's footsteps descending the steps.

"R-R-R-RONALD, is, is that you man?" I managed to gasp out. "HA, ha, ha, ha!"

"Sure it is Mr. Gimble, who else would it be?" Ronald asked in response and took my blindfold off me.

"Time for your five minute break," he said and turned off the record player.

The feathers stopped spinning and stopped tickling my feet.

"OH, thank you, thank you Ronald," I said softly, sitting there and stinking in my sweat.

"Thirsty?" Ronald asked me, holding up a bottle of mineral water.

"Sure am man," I replied. "B-but I have to piss so bad I don't think it's a good idea to..."

But before I could finish the sentence, Ronald had one hand in my sweat-sopped hair and was holding the bottle forcefully to my trembling lips. He pulled my head back and forced me to guzzle down the entire quart of water. As I glugged and chugged miserably my cock pounded long, hard and aching in my suit trousers.

"Now, what was that you said about having to piss Mr. Gimble?" Ronald asked me fiendishly, after the water was all gone.

He put the bottle down on the floor and wiped my wet lips with one of my socks. Smelling it I knew what it was that drove my poor wife crazy about my putrid foot scent. My damned socks did stink at that, yet my cock grew harder still at the scent of them as Ronald wiped my lips with one of them. When he was done wiping my lips he put my sock back in his pocket and crouched down at the bulge in my suit pants.

"Man, look at that," Ronald panted, running a hand over my throbbing crotch.

"D-don't you dare you bastard!" I ranted and made the mistake of leaning back in the chair. "AYYY GOD!"

By pulling my chest back it caused the tit clamps to really pull on my poor nipples, sending searing pain throughout my body. Shit, from being tickled for two straight hours and having my tits clamped for so long, every damned part of me was more than sensitized. And from all points, Ronald had no intention of letting me go just yet. I watched helplessly as the guy slowly pulled the zipper down on my suit pants, reached in past my BVDs and brought out my big beefy uncut eight inch cock, along with my big juicy and sweat soaked balls. I grimaced miserably as the guy handled me totally roughly down there.

"Shit, look at the size of this damned executive cock of yours man," Ronald said in awe. "Holy fuck, I didn't think that an average guy like you would have such an enormous piece of man meat like this."

The fucking guy rolled my foreskin up and down the sides of my big cock, sending chills of ecstasy through me. Then, Ronald checked his watch, told me that my break was almost over, held my cock straight out and placed the tip of the empty water bottle over the crown of it.

"Piss you handsome fucking executive," Ronald commanded.

With no choice other than to do as I was told, and because I had to so very badly, I pissed. I pissed long, hard, heavy, frothy and yellow into the quart-sized bottle. Relief filled me as my bladder drained. My cock remained super hard, making it difficult to piss in the bottle. When I was done pissing I saw that I had really pissed a good amount into the bottle. Ronald began stroking my hard cock.

"OHHH GAAWWWD, no, oh no, not this you bastard!" I ranted angrily. "Fucking going to make me shoot my damned load you pervert!"

Thoughts of my wife filled my head as I shot a big hefty load of creamy executive sperm into the bottle along with my piss.

"OHHH GOD, you pervert, you fucking bastard!" I seethed at Ronald, my poor nipples really coming to stinging life in the tit clamps now. "AYYY SHIT!"

When I was done spurting my load Ronald put the bottle back down on the floor, leaving my cock and balls hanging out of my suit pants. The tip of my cock disappeared under my slimy foreskin and I writhed and bucked miserably in the chair as the clamps tormented my poor tits worse than before. I had just learned that when a guy's tits are clamped and he shoots a load the pain in his tits intensifies about a hundred fucking times.

"G-get those things off my tits you bastard!" I demanded.

But Ronald was not one of my office personnel and did not have to take orders from me. And let's face it, I was in no position to be giving him orders. Ronald stood up, stepped behind me and tied my tie back over my eyes, blindfolding me again.

"Ronald, please," I pleaded softly, choking on my tears.

"Ready for another hour of being tickled Mr. Gimble?" Ronald asked as tied the blindfold over my eyes.

"Ronald, please, please, let me go man," I begged as I then heard him move toward the record player.

He turned it on and once again my bare feet were being tickle tortured.

"OHHH no, no, no, oh no, not again you slimy fuck!" I gasped. "Ha, ha, ha, ha, ha!"

"I'm going to go for a drive to get some more stuff that I can use on you Mr. Gimble," Ronald said, giving one of my big toes a squeeze and a fast suck. "See you soon. Enjoy yourself."

"NO, no, don't leave me alone again you fucking pervert!" I ranted through clenched teeth. "Ha, ha, ha, ha! OHHH GAWD!"

"Before the day is out I'll lick your feet for a while," I heard Ronald say as he ascended the steps again. "That should have you feeling real good. God, I'm sure glad I saw you in Alex's office that day."

"J-just what I'll need, to have my damned stinking feet licked by a pervert like you, ha, ha, ha, ha! OHHH GOD!"

Again, the sound of the basement door slamming shut...

I was again alone and being horribly tickle tortured...

"HA, HA, HA, HA, HA, HA!" I shrieked. "TH-this is too much now! OHHH SHIIITTT!"

This time as I was tickle tortured, my thoughts wandered back to the day when my wife and I were in Alex's Real Estate office. We were seated side by side at his desk as we gave him our information and what we were looking for in the way of a house. Alex, a young real estate agent with dark hair and small eyes sat at his desk and wrote our information on a legal pad. I sat there dressed in a charcoal gray colored suit, white shirt, black silk tie, my black wingtips and calf length black cotton dress socks. I didn't recall seeing Ronald in the office, but then, my attention was focused on the task at hand. My eyes didn't wander around the office even once. My wife and I held hands as we sat there relating information to Alex as he wrote. I recalled slipping my feet around the legs of the chair. Ronald said that that really had caught his eye. Was that my damning moment? Jeez, and all because I have such damned cute feet.

"HA, ha, ha, ha, ha!" I laughed as I thought about the day at Alex's desk in the Real Estate office.

As the hour crawled by I was again bathed in sweat and reeking of it by then. When this hour was over I would have been tickled for three straight hours. Un-fucking-thinkable, but it was happening! And the pervert had gone out to get more stuff that he planned to use on me. My mind raced with the possibilities of the stuff that he would be bringing to use on me. My God, was I in a pickle or what? My cock was again piss-filled and hard, pointing straight up at the ceiling. I could feel droplets of pre cum and beads of piss oozing from my side sexy slit, my foreskin pulled back on my erection. GOD, the fucking guy had jacked me off, made me shoot my load. I could not believe this was happening!

"HOOO, HOOO, ha, ha, ha, ha!" I laughed, gasping for breath at that point.

By the time the hour was up, I wasn't even laughing coherently anymore. More like the sounds of heavy heaving and dry gasps were coming from me as the feathers spun and spun and spun and spun against my poor bare feet. I didn't even hear the sound of the basement door being opened and then closed. The only indication that Ronald had returned was the fact that the record player was switched off and the feathers stopped tickling me. I sat there heaving, gasping, sweating and even crying as the guy again took the sopping wet blindfold off me.

"Man, only three hours and already you're pretty wasted Mr. Gimble," Ronald said jovially, leaving my tie turned blindfold dangling around my neck. "I just love seeing how much being tickled a guy can take."

"PL-please," I whispered, looking up at him with my head hanging back.

"Man, I have to do something to bring you around Mr. Gimble," Ronald said, holding up a medium sized brown paper bag. "I'm really glad I went and got all this stuff. It seems like you laughed yourself into a stupor."

"JEEZ, I wonder why..." I whimpered.

Ronald put the paper bag down on the floor and brought out a fresh quart-sized bottle of mineral water. He gingerly held it to my trembling lips.

"N-no water, no water man," I whimpered miserably. "I-I have to piss like crazy already."

"I don't want you dehydrating on me Mr. Gimble," Ronald said and pressed the tip of the bottle to my lips, forcing me to sip the water down. "I'm just having loads of fun with you, I don't want to wind up having to take you to an emergency room. As for the need to piss, not to worry, I have just what you need for that in the bag."

And so, with one hand behind my sweaty neck and the other hand holding the water bottle to my lips Ronald forced me to swig down the cold water. With each sip the need to piss intensified. My nipples were beyond numb and stinging at that point. I didn't know at that moment, but they would feel even worse when Ronald finally took the clamps off them.

"Come on Mr. Gimble, down the hatch," Ronald said, sounding impatient. "Your breaks are only five minutes long and I have to start getting you tickled again. I'm going to work you for another two straight hours again."

I sputtered like mad around the tip of the water bottle, water and my spittle flying in all directions and all over my exposed and sweat soaked chest. Ronald's last statement had really brought me up and out of the stupor I had slid into.

"T-two fu-fucking hours more?" I gasped madly. "Y-you have got to be kidding man! This foolishness has gone far enough! I demand that you release me now!"

"Want to go for three straight hours you handsome fuck?" Ronald asked me, holding the water bottle to my lips and squeezing the back of my sweat sopped neck.

Without a word I wrapped my lips angrily around the tip of the bottle. My cock pounded in fear and anger as Ronald fed me gulp after gulp of that damned cold water.

"Not to worry though Mr. Gimble, I'm going to be here for the entire two hours," Ronald said merrily. "It's going to be more than just your cute feet being tickled this time."

I groaned miserably around the tip of the bottle...

Less than a few minutes had gone by and the water bottle was empty.

I had drunk every drop of it and now the need to piss was maddening. My hard cock pointed straight up at the ceiling, twitching with a life all its own. Pre cum and beads upon beads of piss oozed from my slit.

"G-going to have me piss in that bottle now?" I asked Ronald angrily.

"No, not this time Mr. Gimble," Ronald said, stepping over to the record player, the fucking instrument of my torture. "Ready?"

"H-has it been five minutes already man?" I asked very sadly.

"Sure has," Ronald said, glancing at his watch and flicked the switch on the record player.

The blasted feathers spun to life at the 78-RPM speed and in less than a few seconds I was again laughing loudly and uncontrollably.

"OHHH GOD, GOD, ho, ho, ho, ho, ho, ho, ho, OHHH FUCKKK, an-another t-two hours of this and I'll be dead for sure you bastard!" I cackled incoherently. "HA, ha, ha, ha, ha! OHHH GOD, y-you're going to make my wife a widow you bastard! HA, ha, ha, ha, ha!"

As I writhed in the bondage laughing madly my cock twitched around sporadically.

"Two hours of having your cute feet tickled and then some," Ronald said fiendishly and reached into the paper bag he had brought with him.

I nearly screamed in terror when I saw the high-speed electric toothbrush he produced from the bag.

"OHHH GOD, no, no, Ronald please," I crowed desperately as he hunched down at my crotch. "OH GOD, not this!"

The fucking sadist flicked the electric toothbrush on and I watched in agony as the dry bristles whirred to life. They seemed to be vibrating at more than a hundred miles per hour. Slowly, and with a look of utter delight on his face, Ronald brought the whirring bristles close to my cock.

"OHHH GOD, ha, ha, ha, ha, oh no, you bastard! I shrieked.

Ronald grabbed my big sweaty testicles and held them tight as he gently pressed the vibrating bristles of the toothbrush against the shaft of my hard and throbbing cock.

"OOO SSSHHHIIITTT!" I roared and spurts of piss erupted madly from my slit, landing messily and gunge-like on my exposed upper torso. "AYYY GOD, got, got me fucking pissing all over myself, FUCK!"

Ronald chuckled heartily as the scent of my thick yellow stream mixed with the sweat all over me. The feathers spun and spun against my bare, smelly, tickled feet, pushing me closer and closer to the edge of insanity.

"WH-why me?" I blurted as the bristles of the toothbrush heated up my poor cock.

Ronald held tightly to my aching balls and moved the vibrating bristles of the toothbrush all over the shaft of my cock. I pissed like a fucking madman all over myself, hating myself for it, yet unable to control my flow. When Ronald moved the bristles over my wide slit I thought for sure that I would go completely crazy for sure. I thought I was done pissing, but oh man, those vibrating bristles against my sexy slit caused more and more and more AND MORE piss to erupt from me. I sat there laughing and pissing my head(s) off.

"HA, ha, haaa, haaa, ha, ha, ha!" was all I could say.

I sputtered and garbled gibberish when Ronald let go of my balls and pressed the vibrating bristles against them. If I weren't handcuffed to that damned chair I was sure I would have flown right the fuck out of it. Damned electric toothbrush was cooking my poor nuts. Ronald began stroking my cock in and out of my foreskin as he tortured my poor testicles with the toothbrush.

"Damn, that is so sexy," Ronald commented admiring my uncut cock as it slid in and out of my foreskin. "Fuck, the way I'm working your nuts, cooking them in your sac, should get a good hefty load of executive jazz out of you Mr. Gimble."

No sooner were the words out of Ronald's mouth the cum was spewing from my slit.

"OOOHHH GODDD, AAAYYYRRR!" I panted and screamed loudly as I shot and shot my second load, this time all over myself.

What a mess of sweat, piss and cum I smelled like. Ronald stroked me and stroked me and stroked me and fucking stroked me, driving me crazier and crazier as I shot rope upon rope of creamy executive jazz for him. The tickling sensations on my feet and nuts and my orgasm all combined had sent me into a state of high euphoria. I was out of my mind with ecstasy and pain at the same time.

"OOO SSSHHHIIITTT, g-got me creaming, creaming like a bitch in hea-heat," I stammered stupidly.

When I was done shooting my load Ronald let go of my cock and took the electric toothbrush away from my nuts. He watched in awe as my slimy cock softened and shriveled and slid back into my foreskin.

"God, I love that," he whispered.

I was glad for him that he loved my uncut cock so much, but as for me I was in agony. Once again, after having shot my load the tit clamps were driving me crazy with stinging and numbing pain. My poor, poor nipples were swollen to twice their normal size at that point and felt really heavy on my chest. As if reading my mind, Ronald sidled over to my chest area and unclipped the clamps from my nipples.

"AHHHRRR, JEEEZ," I ranted through clenched teeth and balled my cuffed hands into sweaty fists as the pain of the blood rushing back through my nipples was intense and just about unbearable. "YOU, you fucking sick bastard!"

Ronald leaned forward and as I continued to laugh my head off he greedily slurped one of my erect over-sized nipples into his mouth.

"OOOHHH GOD, fucking de-fucking-generate!" I ranted as the guy began really slurping and sucking heartily at my nipple. "HA, ha, ha, ha, ha! F-fucking fucks, now you're eatin' my damned tits! AHHH, ha, ha, ha, ha..."

Looking down I watched as Ronald methodically and almost professionally worked my nipple with his lips, tongue and teeth. My cock began to grow and slide slowly from my foreskin. FUCK! There was no denying that the fucking guy was driving me wild, forcing me to a new skyscraper of an erection. Within a few minutes, my cock was standing up, fully at attention, and rigid and pointing at the ceiling. After a good fifteen minutes or so Ronald stopped working my nipple and flicked the electric toothbrush back on. The sound of it whirring to life filled me with dread. As Ronald brought the vibrating bristles toward my overly erect and numbly tingling nipples, I roared with laughter and begged him not to torture my nipples with the toothbrush.

"HOOO, ho, ho, ho, ho, ho, ho!" I chortled angrily. "PL-please man, no, no! Oh God no!"

My feet were by now a sweaty stinking mess as the spinning feathers tickled and tickled and tickled them. But when Ronald pressed the vibrating bristles against the tip of one of my sore nipples I nearly did fly out of that damned chair I was trapped in.

"HOOOHHH!" I shrieked in uncontrollable laughter. "HOOO GODS, y-you miserable fucker! D-don't be tickling my tits, OOOHHH GOD RONALD!"

Ronald slowly and meanly alternated running the hot vibrating bristles over and over my poor nipples. The tips of them became super hard and I could feel them tingling and burning on my chest as Ronald tickled them more and more.

"HA, ha, ha, ha, ha!" I screamed. "TH-this is sick torture you bastard!"

I wriggled my toes and open and closed my cuffed hands involuntarily as I was tickle tortured and tickle tortured. By the time the fucking guy stopped tickling my nipples with the electric toothbrush, they were beyond swollen. Ronald flicked his tongue over the sides of one of them a few times. They were highly sensitized so the slightest touch on them drove me batty. FUCK, FUCK, and the guy had managed to get me all worked up in the cock again... via my tits and tickling... of all the blasted things...

"HA, ha, ha, ha, ha!" I laughed miserably. "N-never laughed so much in my life!"

"And there's plenty more coming, you handsome fuck," Ronald said meanly before finally turning off the toothbrush.

While I sat there having my poor feet tickle tortured Ronald squatted down at the side of my crotch and busied himself toying with my big uncut meat stick. He was in awe of it once more as he slid it in and out of my foreskin.

"HA, ha, ha, ha, HAH, HAH, HAH, HAHHH, OH GOD, I-leave my cock alone you pervert!" I seethed, the tempo of my laughter increasing as the sensations of Ronald stroking my cock send chills beyond chills through my being tickled being.

But as the guy stroked my slimy guy in and out and in and out of my foreskin there was no doubt I would soon shoot a third load, that's how worked up the fucker had me. As Ronald stroked me and stroked me and as I laughed my head off louder and louder I again thought of my wife. She also has a fascination with my uncut cock. She loves stroking me in and out of my foreskin and watching me cum for her. My wife, fuck, she can play with my cock for hours before we get down to the business at hand. She calls it foreplay, stroking me and making me cum once and then stroking me up to a new erection and having me fuck the tar out of her. I call it ecstasy. But when Ronald slurped the tip of my cock between his lips and just held it there I thought I would lose my mind for sure.

"HA, ha, ha, ha, ha, OOOHHH GOODDD!" I screeched madly. "OH you fucked up fucking fucker!"

The way that Ronald had the tip of my cock between his lips and not moving, there was no way, NO FUCKING WAY I could shoot my load. Fucking fucks, this time the guy was going to make me wait. The sound of my raucous laughter filled the room, my damned tickle prison...

Ronald had the patience of a saint and the fiendishness of a devil that was for sure. As I sat there laughing and laughing the guy simply held my hard pulsing cock tip gingerly between his lips.

"F-FUCKER, ha, ha, ha, ha, OOOHHH GODS in the heavens and devils in hell, you bastard!" I roared.

When Ronald poked his tongue tip into my wide sexy slit and swirled it around in there, chills that felt akin to electricity coursed through every part of my body. MY GOD, I was beyond sensitized at that point. I needed to shoot my third load, I needed to stop laughing for longer than five-minute intervals and I needed to be out of this fucked up situation. But Ronald was having way too much fun with me. I knew as he held my cock tip between his lips and tongue and teased my slit that I was still in for more nastiness.

"HA, ha, ha, ha, ha!" I roared loudly and miserably.

When Ronald finally took his lips off my cock tip and I still could not cum, a feeling more than frustration consumed and overwhelmed me. My poor erection bobbed around between my legs, twitching like crazy, my big juicy balls resting atop the crotch area of my sweat soaked suit trousers.

"HA, ha, ha, ha, ha, HAH!" I laughed crazily, as my bare feet were tickled and tickled and tickled and tickled. L-LOOK at that, just look at that, my, my cock is so hard... but I can't, HA, HA, HA, HA, I can't cum, oh God, what a joke on me... and it's not funny!"

"Well Mr. Gimble, the first hour of this two hours is almost over," Ronald said, glancing at his watch. "You should consider yourself lucky that I'm honest about your time frames and your five minute breaks."

"WH-when is this going to stop?" I managed to garble. "WH-when are you going to let me the fuck out of here?"

"Now Mr. Gimble, you know the answer to that question as well as I do," Ronald replied, squatting next to me and tweaking one of my sore nipples hard. "You told Alex you were going to take the entire day off. At the end of the workday I'll release you."

"HA, HAH, HAH, HA, HAH, HA, HAH, HA, HA!" I laughed in stupid reply. "Y-you mean we-we're going to be at this shit all, all fucking day? OHHH shit man! What a thing to do to a poor guy, of all the blasted things!"

As I sat there helpless the reality of a long, long day of being tickle tortured settled meanly into my executive mind. This would be the greatest challenge of my career, that was for sure, DAMN.

Approximately five minutes into the second hour of that time frame Ronald produced two clip-on clothespins from his bag of tricks. He clipped them tightly onto my jutted up nipples and amid my laughter and screams of pain, he next produced a few cotton tipped Q-tips from the bag. I laughed and watched as the fucking prankster knelt on his haunches, right near my damned deep and sweat sopped belly button.

"HARRRHHH, HARRR," I laughed, not even able to form words of protest at that moment as Ronald moved the tips of two of the Q-tips toward my belly button.

I wanted to tell him not to tickle torture my belly button, that having that tickle tortured combined with my feet being tickled and my nipples now being clothes-pinned would surely put me over the edge. But alas, I could not even form the words of complaint as I helplessly laughed and laughed and laughed and laughed some more. And even if I could form the words to beg my captor not to tickle torture my belly button, I was sure he would have ignored me. Ronald was having too much fun torturing the fuck out of me to stop at that point...

"AYYYRRR!" I shrieked loudly and throatily with my head tossed back as Ronald slid the tips of the Q-tips into my belly button, pressing hard. "AHHHRRR, HA, HA, HA, HA!"

Ronald pressed the tips of the Q-tips hard against the inside of my belly button and a stinging pain of pressure seared through me and tickled me to the core of my being at the same damned time.

"HAAARRHHH, HARRRHHH, OHHH GAWWWD," was all I could say before I was off on yet another laughing jag. "HA, ha, ha, ha!"

I writhed and bobbed stupidly in my chair prison, sweat literally flying off me now. As I bobbed up and down on the chair the clothespins on my nipples jiggled madly, pulling meanly on my poor sore nips. I was screaming in pain, laughter and from being more than totally and overwhelmingly sensitized. I needed to shoot that load. My God, my cock was hard and aching like I could not believe. Even after having shot those first two loads, I was hornier than a bitch in heat. Somehow being tickle tortured, made to laugh uncontrollably and being sexually teased all had a profound effect on my cock.

Then, with a maniacal looking grin on his face, Ronald pressed the Q-tips harder in my belly button. When he swirled them around in there I guffawed louder yet.

"PL-PLHHH..." I sputtered, not able to form one single word.

I was dizzy as hell, lightheaded and thought for sure that I would pass out any moment. Unfortunately though, I didn't. Shit, I couldn't even escape that way.

"My God, I wonder how that pretty wife of yours would feel seeing you this way Mr. Gimble," Ronald said in awe, taking the Q-tips away from my belly button. "When I send you home to her tonight you are going to be one wiped out super executive that is for sure."

He seemed to study the tip of one of the Q-tips as I sat there laughing my head off. When he moved the tip of the Q-tip toward my wide sexy slit I nearly went totally berserk.

"N, n..." was all I could say as the fucking guy slid the tip of the Q-tip into my cock slit. "OHHH!"

As Ronald swiveled the damned Q-tip around and around in my slit the soundproof basement was filled with the sounds of my screams and laughter, as I shook, trembled, gasped and panted wildly. I watched in agony as Ronald slid the Q-tip further and further into my slit, swiveling it around as it went, fucking tickling me in there... OH THE SHAME...

"HAAARRRHHH, ha, ha, ha, ha!" I laughed insanely.

"Oh yeah, look at your cock opening eating up this Q-tip Mr. Gimble," Ronald laughed and grabbed my sweaty and juicy balls.

I was ready and he knew it. The guy had cooked me tickle-wise long enough. He yanked the Q-tip out of my slit, leaned down, and holding my balls tight he wrapped his lips and mouth around my throbbing cock.

"HHHUUUHHH, OOOHHH," I gasped as Ronald sucked me slowly. "OOOHHH, ha, ha, ha!"

It was one of the most intense orgasms of my life there was no denying it. Ronald sucked me and sucked me and sucked me and sucked me some more, gulping down my hot creamy executive load, not losing a single drop of it. Being tickled, having my nipples clothes-pinned, being sucked and shooting my load all at once sent me into a state of a tailspin I can only describe as overdrive. My head spun, my teeth itched and every other part of me was more than alive. My heart pounded like mad as Ronald continued sucking me, even AFTER I had shot my damned load.

"NO, no, no, no, no," I managed to say.

I grimaced miserably and sweat trickled down my forehead and into my eyes and I watched through blurred vision as the insatiable pervert went on and on sucking me. Fuck, it felt like some sort of suction device had been hooked up to my poor cock. Ronald held tightly to my balls. Obviously he planned to drain them real well...

After I shot my third load Ronald continued bobbing his mouth up and down on my cock, driving me totally stir crazy as he sucked me...

"OOOHHH SHIT, SHIT..." I rasped, as my slimy cock was beyond sensitive after having shot that third load.

I hadn't even had a moment to get soft, fuck; the guy was sucking me up to a forced tingling and numbing erection. He made a funnel of the tip of my foreskin and swiveled and whirled his tongue around in there, sending shockwaves through me.

"HA, ha, ha, ha, ha, HAR, HAR!" I laughed in a high pitched tone.

I clenched my teeth and could not, COULD NOT believe it, because the fucking guy was about to force a fourth load out of creamy executive jazz out of me, and so fucking soon after having just shot a third load. I bucked, screamed and laughed my head off some more as the guy delighted in sucking me, licking my foreskin and tormenting the fucking fucks out of me. I could not stop laughing, couldn't stand the numbing tingling in my cock as the pervert gulped down my juices and could not deal with the pain in my poor clothes-pinned nipples.

When I was done spewing that mess of jazz, Ronald let my cock slowly slip from his mouth. The fucker gave my foreskin a few licks and slurps for good measure. Then, he leaned back on his haunches and watched as the tickle torture machine drove me batty.

"Damn, into your fifth hour of being tickled Mr. Gimble," Ronald said softly. "You sure can take it."

"Y-YOU fucker!" I screamed at him with a smile of insanity on my sweat-sopped face. "This is utter senselessness, pure and fucking simple!"

The rest of the fifth hour seemed to crawl by as Ronald simply sat there on the floor next to me, watching as the Executive Tickle Torture Machine did its work, tickling an executive, me. The basement was filled with the sounds of my laughter, the scent of my sweat and Ronald's gleeful smirk.

"H-How many other g-guys have you had in this position?" I asked him. "HA, ha, ha, ha!"

"A few actually," Ronald said, pulling himself to his knees and moving his face close to my poor trapped and being tickled feet. "But they were the results of bets and wagers. And I kept them in this thing for only a few minutes at a time."

He leaned up and slathered his tongue around one of my big toes. The fucking guy sucked my toe hard, sending chills through me, adding to the chills I was already getting from being tickle tortured.

"I always dreamed of having some young strong handsome executive trapped in this thing for a real long period of time," Ronald said and sucked my big toe again. "I never thought I would get the chance to tickle torture a fucking stud like you Mr. Gimble. And for the better part of a day at that, talk about a real stroke of luck."

He slurped at the tips of my toes, drooled over them and sucked them hard.

"Y-your luck will run out man, m-mark my words," I gasped. "HA, ha, ha, ha, ha, because wh-when I'm out of this thing I am going to make sh-short work of you! HA, ha, ha, ha, ha!"

"When you're out of that thing you're going to need me to carry you home Mr. Gimble," Ronald said meanly, stood up and glanced at his watch. "Five more minutes and then it's break time again. And this is what I'll be using on that big cock of yours during your break time."

That said, Ronald reached into his infernal bag and brought out a jar of blue ice heat rub. I screamed with laughter and utter terror…

Five minutes later Ronald switched off the record player. I breathed a long and loud sigh of relief as the feathers stopped spinning and tickling my poor feet. Ronald took the clothespins off my nipples and I screamed in major agony as the blood rushed furiously back through them.

"TH-this is too much now Ronald," I whispered. "PL-please, c-can't we be done at this point?"

Ronald glanced at his watch.

"But Mr. Gimble, it's only a little after three thirty," Ronald said merrily and ran three fingertips under my chin. "The workday ends at five. But think about this, you have less than two more hours of tickling time to endure."

"OH God," I whispered woefully

Unbelievably, my cock was again hard and piss-filled, standing painfully erect between my legs and pointing straight up at the ceiling. Just as Ronald would have wanted it, and my nipples were also beyond erect, swollen to twice their size. I glanced down at the floor where my shoes were and looked longingly at them. Next to my wingtips was the mineral water bottle that contained my piss and a mucky mixture of globs and globs and globs of my cum. What a sight that was let me tell you.

"Thirsty?" Ronald asked me, opening a fresh bottle of mineral water.

"Yeah, and hungry you bastard, I haven't eaten since breakfast," I replied angrily.

"Well, I think we'd better just stick with the water for now Mr. Gimble," Ronald said, placing a hand behind my neck and holding the tip of the bottle to my lips. "The way I have you laughing so hysterically here you're liable to upchuck any food that I give you. Tell you what though, seeing as you've been such a good sport about all this I'll take you out to dinner when we're done."

I stopped sipping the water and looked at him maddeningly.

"G-good sport?" I asked the guy. "After you managed to trick me into this thing I don't see where I had all that much of a choice Ronald."

Ignoring me, Ronald fed me more and more water. My stomach gurgled and beads upon beads of piss slithered from my slit. When the water was done, Ronald put the empty bottle on the floor and picked up the jar of blue ice heat rub.

"OH God Ronald, PL-please d-don't slather that stuff on my cock man," I gurgled as he took the lid off the jar.

Smiling wickedly, Ronald dipped two fingers into the slimy looking blue gel liquid and then ran those two fingers over and over and over just the tip of my cock. I broke out in goose-bumps as the stuff automatically did its work, heated up yet was cold and numbing at the same time.

"OOO SHHHIIIT," I garbled throatily.

Ronald dipped his fingers into the jar again and this time rubbed the tips of them over and over and up and down the back of my erect cock shaft.

"YAHHH, ooohhh you bottom feeder," I gasped and tossed my head back, heaving and bucking wildly in the chair. "OHHH GAAWWDD, this, this is fucking driving me out of my mind man!"

Needless to say, my erect cock was beyond numb, more than tingling and more than burning with the icy heat.

More beads upon beads of piss trickled from my slit and Ronald was attempting to jack me off yet again at the same time. Fucking guy really knew how to drive a big-time executive like me crazy.

"OOOHHH GAAAWWD, Ronald, if, if that offer of buying me dinner when this is over was true I-I'm going to want a stea-steak dinner man," I gasped and looked back down at the guy as he worked my erection slowly, oh so slowly.

"Your five minutes are almost up Mr. Gimble, you'd better cum soon, or at least piss good and hard, after all the times I made you cum already I have to wonder if you'll be able to spew some more," Ronald said mockingly. "If neither happens your cock is going to be feeling very frustrated when I start the tickling machine again."

"Y-you fucking smart ass, work my cock faster," I panted, not believing what I had just said to my kidnapper, GOD!

Ronald simply kept moving his fingertips slowly up and down and up and down the back of my cock shaft. He watched as more piss slithered from my slit.

"Best to let you piss and get the machine going again," Ronald said and stopped stroking me.

"OHHH GOD, no, no, Ronald, plea-please," I pleaded as my cock stood overly erect and super-numbed between my legs.

Ronald picked up the empty water bottle, held my cock straight out and put the tip of the bottle over the tip of my cock.

"PISS," Ronald commanded, holding tightly to my poor numb cock, but not stroking it.

I took a hearty breath and did as he said and pissed. I managed to piss and piss long and heavy into the water bottle, knowing that the mean bastard was not going to allow me to cum this time, painful as it might have been if I did. When I was done pissing almost a minute later, Ronald took the bottle away from my cock tip and let go of my cock. My manhood again pointed straight up at the ceiling, super erect and super numb. Ronald checked his watch.

"One minute and a half to go," Ronald said. "Aren't you glad I'm so honest?"

"Yeah, thrilled," I said dejectedly and made the mistake of licking my lips.

"Still thirsty Mr. Gimble?" Ronald asked me, holding up the water bottle I had just pissed into. "Well, I don't have any more water, so this will have to do."

Before I could protest or even say a word the guy grabbed my nose, squeezed it tight, tilted my head back and forced me to guzzle down my rancid and hot piss.

"GGGRRRMMMFFF!" I sputtered angrily as my piss filled my mouth and slopped down my throat.

"Down the hatch Mr. Gimble," Ronald said merrily.

He forced me to drink it all down and then put the bottle down on the floor.

"Y-you mangy bastard!" I ranted at him as he stepped over to the record player. "You sick fuck, you made me drink my damned piss!"

Smiling, Ronald held up a finger and gestured toward the other water bottle that was filled with my piss and cum.

"Keep carrying on like that and I'll make you drink that one down too," Ronald said in a reprimanding tone of voice. "Now, you have exactly one hour and fifteen minutes of tickling time to endure."

That said, Ronald switched on the record player and once again, the feathers were spinning and spinning over my bare feet.

"HA, ha, ha, ha, ha, ha, HAH, HAH, HAH, HAH!" I snarled loudly.

"AH, just love to hear you laugh Mr. Gimble," Ronald said happily.

As I sat there helplessly, being tickle tortured again Ronald picked up the jar of blue ice rub and slathered more of it over the tip of my cock, all over my shaft and this time even all over my balls.

"YARRRHHH, OOOHHH, GOD, n-no man," I pleaded. "HA, ha, ha, ha, ha!"

The fucking guy really got his jollies from my balls aching as he liberally applied the blue ice rub to them. He purposely squeezed the fuck out of my poor nut sac, really getting it icy hot and burning. I screamed crazily to no avail, laughing and crying at the same damned time. My cock and balls were beyond tingling as the icy heat rub numbed them. When Ronald brought the long goose feather out of his bag of tricks and started moving it toward my wide sexy slit, I started crying even harder, laughing uncontrollably at the same time...

"OOO, n-no, no, no," I panted as Ronald moved the tip of the feather into my cock slit. "OOOHHH GAAAWWDDD, ha, ha, ha!"

I laughed, bucked and writhed in the chair as Ronald meanly twirled the tip of the feather in my slit. The need at that point to shoot my executive load was overwhelming, and the fucking guy tickling my cock slit was making the situation hundreds of times worse. I guffawed uncontrollably as new beads of piss slithered from my cock hole. He then moved the feather over my swollen sensitized nipples, rubbing just the very tips of them, sending ticklish shockwaves through my upper body.

"YARRRHHH OHHH you slimy fucker!" I chortled. "HA, ha, ha, ha!"

My toes seemed to wiggle involuntarily and my fingers clenched and opened as Ronald teased and teased my tits with the long goose feather, sliding it up and down my torso, tickled my ribs and even poked the tip of it into my belly button. All this while my poor feet were being tickle tortured. My head spun away at that point and all I heard was the sound of insane laughter, my insane laughter...

I leaned my head back, squeezed my eyes shut and just laughed and laughed and laughed...

When it was five o'clock and Ronald turned off the record player, I didn't even realize that I had stopped being tickled. I felt Ronald's tongue slathering over my sweaty bare feet as they still sat trapped in the stocks. I slowly opened my eyes and looked down at the guy as he furiously and hungrily licked the bottoms of my meaty feet.

"Is, is it over?" I whispered; sweat dripping liberally off my face.

"Sure is, Mr. Gimble, and congratulations, you did very well," Ronald said and leaned up to suck my big toes into his mouth.

He sucked my toes heartily and my cock throbbed wildly and hard between my legs.

"Fuck man, that feels so good," I said softly. "H-how many hours did you tickle torture me for man?"

"A little more than five hours Mr. Gimble," Ronald replied and sucked my toes back into his mouth.

I leaned my head back and laughed softly. Fuck, I could not believe I had been had this way. Ronald finished licking my feet and then he opened the stocks. Thanking God I pulled my bare feet out of them and put them on the floor. Sitting there with my bare feet at my sides Ronald unlocked the handcuffs, releasing me from the Executive Tickle Torture Machine.

"Feeling okay?" he asked me, placing his big hands on my shoulders and squeezing them hard, massaging them.

"Yeah, just fucking great," I replied sarcastically. "Fuck man, I smell like a locker room."

"Well, the bathroom is upstairs and fully equipped with soaps, shampoos and towels," Ronald said, helping me to my feet. "I'll show you the rest of the place, you can take a shower and then we'll discuss the price of the house over dinner."

"Fuck man, I cannot believe I'm still planning to do business with you after all this,": I said, bending down to pick up my shoes.

"You'll be doing more than business with me Mr. Gimble," Ronald said, taking me by the upper arm and walking with me toward the stairs. "After you and your wife buy this house you'll have me here quite often to tickle torture you in that thing."

As we walked up the stairs I looked back at the Executive Tickle Torture Machine and I could have sworn that it looked hungry, ready to gobble me up again for more of what I had just endured…

Well, needless to say, my wife and I did buy the house. At the price that Ronald was asking there was no way we could resist it. Ronald privately explained to me that he was giving us the house at such a low price because he wanted something from me in return. I didn't need three guesses to know what that was. The Executive Tickle Torture Machine is still in the basement. My wife got a real kick out of it when she saw it and agreed with Ronald that it could be fun to use at a party. She had no idea how her handsome husband had suffered so miserably in it. So, on the nights when my wife is in her business meetings Ronald comes over and hooks me up in the thing. I have never been tickle tortured for as long as he worked me the first time, only because our time is limited and my wife would be home soon. But, as Ronald pointed out to me, my wife had mentioned a business trip that she had to go on in a month. She would be gone for a week. Over dinner, Ronald told me how he planned to double the tickling time I had endured the first time. As he spoke, he reached across the table, tugged on my tie and rubbed one of his feet against mine under the table. I gulped hard…

The End?

Thinking of Timmy Backman…

Author's Note and Thanks

The story, "Tickling Arthur's Feet" would never have come to life if it were not for a few very important people in my life. First, thanks to Phil, AKA ETUK@AOL.com, (Wherever he may be at this point) a man who calls himself "ExecTickler." When I first saw his invention of the "Executive Tickle Torture Machine" featured on the ROPEJOCK.com website (a now long-gone site) my imagination went into overdrive. Thanks Phil, for inventing such a fiendish and fun device. I hope to see it work someone someday and perhaps even experience it for myself. (Just kidding?) Second, thanks to the artist Franco, (wherever he too may be at this point in time) whose erotic artwork when it comes to tickling and spanking is truly exceptional. His drawings have given me so much inspiration for erotic stories that if I didn't keep notebooks where I write down my ideas for stories I would never remember them all. (Franco's artwork was also featured on the ROPEJOCK.com website.) Third, thank you thank you to Jack, (sadly, now deceased) the webmaster at ROPEJOCK. com. The stories and pictures he featured and many sections on that website inspired me like I cannot even describe. To "Incurable" Ed West, the head man at "Dreamscape" publications. Thanks as always for your fiendish ways and ideas on how to tickle torture a handsome guy. I am looking forward to more of your work very soon. I know how busy you've been. And last, but certainly not least, thank you to that handsome executive on the "B train who was the inspiration for the character of Arthur Gimble in my stories, "Licking Arthur's Feet" and "Tickling Arthur's Feet." You are exceptionally handsome; you look great in those severe business suits you wear and the way you hike those trousers up way over your ankles and shows off your black ribbed nylon dress socks drives me wild bud. I love those feet of yours and could worship and tickle torture them for days. I am sure that if you read this you would know who you are... Thanks to all the guys listed here who inspired this story, I LOVED WRITING it.

Ethan's Feet

Since we met in college, three years ago at this point, I've been taking care of my buddy, Ethan's feet. It's not a job I signed on for, it just sort of landed in my lap it can be said, the same way Ethan's feet have landed in my lap, and countless times at this point. It's a job I love. It began when we were roommates in college. Ethan had been accepted to the prestigious university on a football scholarship and I was majoring in business and business law. Yeah, I was planning on becoming a high-end, high-paid, high silk-socked and tightly neck-tied Wall Street suited executive.

One of the first times I took care of Ethan's feet was shortly after we had become college roommates in our dorm room, which I will get into soon enough, but from the day we met and became roommates it had been decided that I would take care of Ethan's feet on a daily basis. And this would be whether those feet of Ethan's were bare, sandaled, socked, sockless, shoed, sneaker or cleat clad, or *whatever*... I mean, it wasn't even something we had to talk about, *it just was.* Okay, obviously it was mentioned. You can't massage and knead and rub and mouth worship your college roommate's feet without it being talked about a bit, but hey, it worked out for both of us, so what the fuck right?

The first weekend that we were roommates Ethan had gone out on a date on Saturday night with his high school sweetheart, Suzanne, to celebrate his having been accepted to the prestigious college and the fact that he knew, he just KNEW that he was on his way to the NFL, on his football scholarship. While Ethan was out on his date I stayed in our dorm room to study up on some lessons that I had already been assigned by some of my professors during the past week.

I was sitting on the couch in our dorm room when Ethan came in from his date around one AM. I was sitting there taking notes from a text book on business law when Ethan sauntered in, looking happier than a pig in shit, but sober as well. Given that Ethan was an athlete who was looking to a future as a professional footballer with the NFL the guy was totally drug and alcohol free. AND he kept his body in the most tip-top shape by working out four days a week at the gym with weights, and a cardio routine that was almost boot camp worthy.

"Hey buddy, you still up?" Ethan said as he came in, closing and locking the door behind him.

Ethan was dressed real regally in a pale green button down shirt with no tie, black trousers, and lace-up highly shined black cap toe shoes.

"Yeah, can't believe I have all this studying to do and only the first week of classes. College sure isn't high school," I replied and Ethan shoved his keys in his pants pocket. "So, how was your date?"

"Awesome," Ethan said, sat down on the other end of the couch where I was seated, and with no hesitation whatsoever plopped his big size twelve feet in my lap.

I grinned from ear to ear, put the book I was reading from aside and wrapped my fingers and thumbs of both hands around each of Ethan's gigantic feet.

I ran the palms of my hands up and down the fronts and sides of my college roommate's cap toe shoes, lifted them one at a time to my face, and holding them one at a time by his socked ankle, kissed and licked the tips of those cap toes. I sniffed the shoe leather real heartily, squeezed the backs of Ethan's shoes, and after I had set his feet back down in my lap I tugged a few times on Ethan's shoelaces.

"Damn man, you really are some piece of work bud," Ethan said with a chuckle, watching intently as I slowly undid the laces on his shoes, loosened his shoes and began slipping the right sided one off his big foot, shoe store salesman style.

Once the shoe was off his foot and as I was holding it from the bottom, Ethan said, "Worship that shoe bud, and show it the proper respect it deserves."

I smiled real wide, pressed the inside of the shoe over my nose and mouth, and inhaled deeply, over and over and over and over, breathing in the oh so masculine stink of Ethan's foot, his nylon dress sock and manly musty foot odor.

I kept that shoe over my nose and mouth for a few good minutes, until Ethan told me to stop sniffing it and to do the same thing with the left one.

I placed Ethan's right shoe on the floor and got his left one off his foot, the same way I had done with the right one. Once again I placed the inside of Ethan's shoe over my nose and mouth, inhaled deeply and breathed in the scents of it. This time I even spit in the shoe a few times and sucked and licked my saliva from it, really tasting Ethan's feet. After I had had enough of Ethan's left shoe I placed that one on the floor as well and proceeded to wrap my fingers and thumbs of both hands around each of Ethan's enormous socked feet and began massaging them, real hard.

"Yeah, me and Suzanne had a great dinner at Morton's, then we went back to her dorm room for a little Ta tee ta, if you get my drift bud," Ethan chuckled, resuming our conversation about his date as I massaged his socked feet harder. "And now, oh yeah, now nice feet rub and massage to round out the evening, damn, no one's got it better than I do at this college."

"Dude, you did Suzanne in her dorm room?" I asked, massaging and squeezing Ethan's toes, twisting them, kneading them, the musty scent of his nylon socks wafting up at me, the smell not that bad at all, instead it was rather intoxicating to me, an aromatic mixture of feet sweat, nylon socks and leather from his shoes of course. "But that's an all-girl college. You could have gotten in trouble for being there… and Suzanne could have been thrown out and…"

"Dude, *dude,* no worries, we were real careful you know?" Ethan laughed, watching as I massaged his toes and then resumed squeezing and kneading his big feet. "Nothing to worry about there for you, just tend to my feet eh?"

"Sure thing bud," I said, loving for some reason to call him "bud." "But man, I don't know if you know or realized it, but *you are* def wearing the wrong color dress socks here. With the outfit you're wearing your size twelves should be attired in black nylon numbers and you're wearing brown nylon socks. What's up with that anyway?"

Ethan grinned and said, "Suzanne said the same thing after we got undressed in her dorm room. I guess I was in such a rush to get to her that when I got dressed earlier I didn't realize I had picked out the wrong color socks, and maybe, *just maybe,* dude, given *your* penchant for my feet, MAYBE I did it on purpose, you know, on a subconscious level maybe?"

"Why?" I asked. "So I could point it out for you bud?" I asked and tugged the nylon material of Ethan's socks away from his toes… and then slid one hand under Ethan's right sided trousers leg and found the top of his sock, mid-calf length.

"Maybe, I know how you love *everything* about my damned feet, I mean, look at how you worshipped my shoes just a few moments ago, so yeah, maybe I wore the wrong color socks so you would have something to initiate a conversation about tonight where my big dogs are concerned," Ethan said snidely as I began slowly, so fucking slowly tugging his sock down his calf, using the fingers of both hands as I did so.

"So you uh, left your socks on when you did Suzanne in her dorm room bud?" I asked as I then slid Ethan's right sock over his ankle and then off his meaty sweaty foot.

"Yeah, sure as hell did, after *she* pointed out the fact that I was wearing brown socks instead of black ones I thought it would be fun to sex her down while I was still wearing them," Ethan replied. "I don't know why man, but it just drove me on all the more while I was fucking the tar out of her to have my damned socks on."

"Fuck, that's so ex-New York Governor Eliot Spitzer," I said and we both laughed. "You remember him, right bud? The governor who was caught having sex with prostitutes... the one who left his black mid-calf length dress socks on while doing the duty?"

"Yeah, fucking Spitzer made it classic for a dude to leave his dress socks on while fucking," Ethan said, still grinning.

That said I held Ethan's wrinkled and smelly sock up in front of my face, the sight of it dangling there mesmerizing to me.

FUCK, how special and intimate was this, to be holding one of my handsome buddies socks up after having just taken it off his foot myself? How many fetishists can say they've done that with a buddy of theirs who doesn't even have the same fetish? And how REALLY special was it that that buddy of mine whose sock I was holding up was on his way to the NFL? I had already decided that when Ethan was accepted to the NFL I planned to keep the socks and cleats or sneakers he would be wearing in the game that earned him *that* acceptance.

When Ethan was famous someday and making headlines like Eli Manning and Tom Brady were currently doing, I would be able to say that I had a pair of the footballer's socks and cleats or sneakers from his past.

With my breath coming in short gasps I looked over at Ethan. He smiled real big and said, "Go ahead man, it's a guy thing, OUR special guy thing..." and with that I pressed the toes section of Ethan's brown dress sock against my lips and nose. I scrunched my eyes tightly closed and in ecstasy inhaled the delicious musty aroma of Ethan's sock, planting small and delicate kisses on it as well, just as I had done with his shoes, licking it, loving it, MY GOD, loving it so much.

"Yeah, that's it man, now suck the juice out of my sock," Ethan said as I wrapped my other hand around his bare foot and began sliding his sock into my mouth, toes section first of course, sucking it as I went, scoffing down my buddies nectar.

I opened my eyes and they crossed in my head as I held tightly to Ethan's bare foot with one hand and pushed as much of his sock into my mouth as possible with my other hand. And oh my fucks and oh my God, but my cock was rock hard and a thing alive in my pants as I did so.

Seconds later only the top part of Ethan's brown nylon dress sock was sticking out of my mouth as I chewed ravenously on the rest of it.

"Heh, heh, if anyone told me that when I came to this college that I would have a roommate who was a total freak for my feet I would have said that they were crazy," Ethan chuckled.

I nodded my head up and down; smiling as best I could with the sock crammed in my craw, and looked down at Ethan's one bare foot and one still brown socked foot in my lap...

"Go ahead man, go for the other one, just like you did with my shoes, it's just as delectable as the one in your mouth already," Ethan said, sounding a bit commanding.

Once more I wrapped both my hands around Ethan's size twelves and began again massaging, squeezing and kneading the life out of them. On his bare foot I twisted and turned his toes, tugged hard on them as if they were cocks and as if I was masturbating them. I did the same thing to his toes on his still socked foot...

"Fucking heady, heady, bud, please don't stop," Ethan pleaded softly. "After my time with Suzanne THIS is a great fucking way to cap off the evening. I fucked the fuck out of her and now my cock is getting hard all over again from you working my feet and seeing you chewing on my damned dress sock of all things."

I nodded my head up and down and as I had done with Ethan's right sided sock I did the same thing now with his left sided one, still chewing away on the sock that was in my mouth. My cock grew hard as steel...

When I found the top section of Ethan's left sock I began slowly tugging it down his calf, heaven man, sheer fucking heaven, the feel of that thin material nylon sock against Ethan's muscular rock hard calf was an erotic contrast.

"Yeah, that's it man, take my other sock off me now, and after all the pungent good taste of my first one is done you can take it out of your mouth and slide the other one in for more good eating," Ethan teased, sounding so mocking, yet it was driving me sexually batty.

I slowly peeled Ethan's left-sided brown sock off his foot, leaving it momentarily around the section of his foot just under his toes and chewed more on the sock that was in my mouth, and massaged and kneaded the guy's feet in my lap real HARD, not wanting to let go of them. Ethan leaned his head back, grunted and groaned and I was able to see the massive sized erection he was sporting in his black trousers...

A few scant moments later I slowly extracted Ethan's right sided sock from my mouth, dropped it on the couch and got his left sock the rest of the way off his foot. I looked at him pleadingly.

"Yeah, do it man, go for it, I know you love it and I love seeing you do it, paying homage to my socks the way you do," Ethan said softly.

Again I began inserting one of Ethan's socks into my mouth, chewing on it as I went...

We stayed on that couch till nearly three AM, me massaging Ethan's bare feet as I chewed on his socks, twisting his toes, rubbing his curvy sexy arches, soothing his hard heels... and driving him and myself crazy. When we finally called it a night I heard Ethan shooting a load in the bathroom as I lay under the sheets of my bed, stroking my own erection as well, the taste of Ethan's socks still in my mouth as I did so...

And to think, we had only been roommates a week at that point...

At that moment I could only imagine what the next four years would be like for me and Ethan.

As I said, Ethan and I met in college three years ago at this point. On the September morning that Ethan and I first met in what would be our dorm room for the next four years it was unseasonably warm out, nearly ninety degrees and just about one hundred percent humidity. I was glad that the college had air conditioning in the dorm rooms.

Ethan arrived in the dorm room five minutes after I had gotten there that morning. I was wearing blue jeans, sneakers and a light blue tee shirt from the Gap, with the word GAP emblazoned across the front of it.

"Hey there, good morning, you must be Chandler Stevenson," I heard someone say from behind me as I was setting down a piece of luggage.

I turned and saw Ethan standing there, he dressed more appropriately for the weather we were having. The guy was clad in cargo shorts, a tank-top and brown, what I call Jesus Christ style sandals.

"Yes, that's me, Chandler Stevenson," I replied, as Ethan set down two pieces of luggage and I took in his green eyes, light brown hair and well-muscled, well-toned football player work of art body. "You must be Ethan, Ethan McDonald?"

"Guilty as charged," Ethan replied, and we shook hands real tight and vigorously.

AND as I shook hands with my new college roommate I could not help it, it seemed, as my eyes wandered down to his sandaled feet. Seeing the straps on the sandals the way they were hugging Ethan's gigantic dogs was mesmerizing... from the first moment I saw them.

"So I hear the dorm room has two bedrooms," I said, quickly tearing my eyes away from Ethan's feet, but too late actually, seeing as the guy had obviously noticed me looking at them as if transfixed. "You can have first choice of either one. They both have air conditioning at least."

"Yeah, unlike out here in the common area, huh?" Ethan asked, running the palm of a hand over his sweaty forehead. "No worries on the sleeping quarters Chandler, I'll take either bedroom. So, what are you studying?"

"Business and business law," I replied. "You?"

"I'm here on a football scholarship dude; while you're headed to Wall Street someday I'll be heading to the NFL," Ethan said jovially.

"Nice, *real nice* that we both have our lives mapped out," I said, loving the way he had just called me bud.

"I've loved football and all things about it since I was a kid," Ethan went on. "And I would think you probably love the stock market and all things business."

"Yeah, I love the idea of challenging business deals, and the suits and ties get to me as well, I suppose, I like the look a lot, and getting a job in the business world will make it so I would have to dress the part," I said. "Most Wall Street dudes hate having to get all dressed and gussied up in suits and ties, but seeing as I've always liked the look I see it as a bonus that goes with the jobs."

Ethan grinned and said, "Yeah, the suits and ties *and* the dress socks and the shoes too huh?"

"Yeah, you could say that I suppose," I replied.

"Ethan grinned wider and said, "Nah, not suppose I could say it, I just said it my new buddy."

With that, and with an expression of slyness now on his handsome puss Ethan stepped to the door of our dorm room, pushed it closed, locked it, glanced down at his sandaled feet, smiled a knowing smile at me, sat down on the couch and propped those sandaled feet of his on the coffee table.

"What?" I asked as Ethan was then looking at me totally expectantly.

"Never mind *what* bud, you know *what*," Ethan said. "You'll find as you get to know me that I'm very direct *and* to the point."

Smiling myself then I hunkered down at the coffee table, directly in front of Ethan's propped up sandaled feet...

He watched knowingly as I wrapped both hands around one of his sandaled feet each. I leaned my face down and pressed my nose and mouth against his visible toes on his right foot.

"Looks like I got me a foot freak for a roommate here at college," Ethan said as I gently kissed his toe tips.

"You don't seem to be saying that like it's a bad thing Ethan," I said and quickly resumed kissing his toe tips, squeezing his sandaled feet as I did so.

The smell of his leather sandals was intoxicating. They smelled as if the future NFL footballer had been wearing them for hours at that point, nice and pungent with his sweaty foot stink all over them.

"Nah, not a bad thing at all new bud," Ethan said, grinning at me like a Cheshire cat. "I *love* having my feet serviced and massaged and kneaded, and yeah, even worshipped, kissed, licked, doesn't matter to me if it's a girl or a guy who does it at that. And to be brutally honest and blunt here, my girlfriend, my high school sweetheart, Suzanne, won't go near my damned feet. She said they smell too musty for her. I'll tell you Chandler, I love having my feet worked so much it's the reason I go for a pedicure every other weekend."

"Yeah, your toenails look real tended to," I said and began undoing the straps on Ethan's sandals.

When I took them off his feet I kissed each of them all over, inside and out and even sucked his sandal straps.

"Fuck, you're not only a freak for feet, you're a freak for a guy's footwear too," Ethan exclaimed, watching practically in awe as I kissed his sandals over and over. "Oh man Chandler, we are going to get along just great buddy."

"Glad to hear that Ethan," I replied, set his sandals down on the floor and wrapped my hands around his now bare feet on the coffee table, really taking in the sight of his gleaming toenails. "Yeah, very nice pedicured toenails bud..."

Then, Ethan crossed his hands up behind his head, smiled, and we both laid big hard-ons, me in my jeans, Ethan in his cargo shorts, and I took a risk and began licking and slobbering over Ethan's toes, and sucked up my saliva real hearty-like, sucking the future NFLers toes as if they were cocks... and Ethan said he felt it in his cock as I sucked his toes...

And that's how it's been since Ethan and I met in college, as stated, three years ago at this point.

For the most part, any time I worked, worshipped, massaged, or did whatever to Ethan's socked or naked feet, that's all it was. In other words, it never went any further, anything sexual we did afterwards, out of each other's sight, like jacking off in our bathroom or under the covers in our separate beds... but one time, oh God, oh my God, one time it went even further. It surprised both of us what happened, and to be honest, neither of us had nor has any regrets...

I had just come in from my classes for that day and Ethan had just gotten in a short while earlier, after a harrowing workout at the instructions of sadistic Coach Zeb Collins.

As I came into the dorm room, closing and locking the door behind me I heard the sounds of throaty groaning. I looked over at Ethan's room, saw that the door was ajar and then heard more groaning. It sounded like the guy was in total pain and agony.

I put my books down on the coffee table and made my way slowly to Ethan's dorm room door.

"Ethan, you okay bud?" I said when I was standing at the slightly open door.

"Naw, not really buddy, fuck," Ethan replied from inside his room.

"Can I, can I uh, can I come in?" I asked.

"Sure, why the fuck not?" Ethan replied and I pushed the door slowly open the rest of the way.

I stepped into Ethan's room and saw that the guy was sitting there on the floor in front of his bed, sopped in sweat, fuck, and his hair was so sweat soaked that it was matted to his head. And lo and fucking behold, he was naked as the day he had been born. I saw his green silk gym shorts with the college football logo etched onto one thigh of them, his white tank-top and sneakers with his calf-length white sweat socks piled up on the floor a few feet from where he was sitting with his legs pressed up against his upper body. AND oh my fucks the way Ethan was sitting there in that position caused his big juicy balls to stick slightly out from between his muscular and oh so shapely thighs.

I have to say that the guy's gym and workout gear looked totally gunged up, as if Coach Collins had made the guy run through oodles of puddles of mud.

"UH, Ethan, you okay bud?" I asked as I took in the sight of the future NFLer.

"AWWW man, what a fucking fucked up workout," Ethan said, leaning back on the bed in all his muscular naked glory. "Coach Collins made us run nearly fifteen goddamned miles on the track, he made us lift weights in the weight room till I thought my boulder-sized biceps would literally rip through the skin on my arms, and then, oh God then, he brought us all down to the army base and made us do *their* obstacle course..."

As he spoke Ethan groaned real throatily, stretching his muscular tree-trunk legs and giant feet out in front of him.

I stood there drinking in the sight of my naked colossally muscular college roommate. And I have to admit my cock was pounding big and hard in the shorts I was wearing.

"AWWW, Chandler, my good buddy, I was so sweated up even wearing my shorts and tank-top and sneakers and socks was too goddamned much for me,' Ethan panted.

"Yeah, I see that," I muttered, drinking in the sight of his semi hard cock as it now hung between his legs as he sat there all stretched out.

"Chandler, Chandler my good buddy, if ever my dogs needed some servicing, *now is the time,*" Ethan moaned, wiggling his toes, not realizing how that was arousing me all the more than I already was.

"UH, yeah, from what I can see, and I can really see it all bud," I said, shucking off the tee shirt I was wearing as I stepped over to Ethan. "From what you just said and from the way you look, you are totally fucking worked over. I mean, your biceps are fucking twitching bud. You really do need some TLC on your feet. And I know for a fact that that *will* relieve the rest of you. I know just how much parts of our bodies are connected to the nerves in our feet and..."

"Okay, okay good buddy, enough with the prattle; let's get to the rattle huh?" Ethan asked demandingly, stood up from the front of his bed, and stretched his god-like body, sweat running off him in what looked like rivers.

His goddamned cock was unashamedly hard at that point and his sweaty testicles were hanging down real low and salacious looking. Ethan stretched a bit more and then sat back down on the floor of his room, a few feet from the bed this time, so he could really stretch out now, which he did, stretching his legs out, real taut-like.

"Oh man Chandler, much as I want to be in the NFL, I doubt I'm going to survive what Coach Collins is putting me through and the rest of the guys on the team at that," Ethan said, hoisting his knees up so his naked feet were flat on the floor now.

My heart and my cock were both racing. Fuck, it felt like there was no room in my shorts that I was wearing for my cock, it was that hard, *that skyscraper erect*. As I stepped over to Ethan I could not believe the thoughts that were suddenly racing through my head. I could not believe what I was thinking of doing to the guy...... instead of just worshipping his smelly robust feet this time out, MY GOD, *the thoughts*, the fucking thoughts that were going through my head buds.

Would the guy still be my friend and roommate if I attempted this?

Fuck, worshipping the dude's feet was one thing, but what I was thinking *now* was a horse of a whole other color, as the saying went.

Ethan was hunkered down on the floor with the palms of his big hands pressed against the floor and his legs spread real wide in front of him, his naked and sweaty feet on total display AND obviously ready for some of my special TLC.

As the guy leaned back a little, arching his head back with his eyes closed now and breathing deeply my breath caught in my throat as I watched his gigantic pecs bounce and twitch involuntarily as his biceps had been doing.

"Fuck, that obstacle course on the army base must be a total mudpack," I said as I then quickly got my shorts and underpants off, knowing I was taking a real chance here, hunkered down in front of Ethan, saw how many patches of mud were on his nearby gear and the scent of male foot sweat, stinking sneaker and sweat sock and leather filled the air around us where Ethan's naked feet were.

The smell emanating from his crotch and exposed ass area was musty as all hell as well. It smelled real funky, like a men's locker room. My cock was at full mast buds, and my balls seemed to be hanging down lower than ever before in my life. Oh fuck, like I said, worshipping my college roommate's feet was one thing, but here, what I was about to do was totally off the Richter scale.

"Yeah, they keep it that way so the recruit's boots will get nice and filthy while they're doing the obstacle course, teaches them to really shine those boots to a high gleam," Ethan responded. "Looks like I'll either have to wash those mud-caked sneakers of mine real well or just invest in a new goddamned pair."

"Fuck, if you invest in a new pair of sneakers bud, I WANT that old pair," I chuckled, hunkered down in front of Ethan and grabbed his aching stinking feet.

"AAAHHH, and there we go good buddy of mine," Ethan panted, his head still arched back and his eyes still closed as I began squeezing his sweaty feet hard, massaging the fuck out of and into them. "Feels so good... so fucking good..."

As I massaged Ethan's feet and leaned forward to bestow kisses on them and sucks on his toes my pre cum dripping erection was aimed at the entrance to Ethan's backdoor. He rocked on the palms of his big hands and I swear, I fucking swear, his asshole looked like it was begging for my cock to fill it.

As I sucked a couple of Ethan's toes on his left foot, really chewed on them to get them feeling good my cock tip touched the outside of his asshole.

"Hey... what the..." Ethan began and his eyes popped open... just as my cock began to enter his wet but tight manhole, inch by ecstatic inch. "Holy fuck buddy, what-what in all hell are you..."

But it seemed as if my steely hard cock had a mind of its own as it slithered it's away deeper into the entrails of Ethan's asshole. I sucked his toes with total gusto, my mouth making slurping sounds as I chugged down the future NFLer's foot stink and massaged his feet even harder... and my cock dug deeper yet into his hole.

"HUUUHHH... oh my God, oh my fucking God Chandler, you-you're, you're fucking me man, you're breeding my goddamned shit chute..." Ethan panted, looking up at me in total shock, his eyes opened wide as saucers as he pressed the palms of his hands harder against the floor.

"Fuck yeah," was all I could say and then slurped a few toes of Ethan's other foot into my greedy mouth, as I began thrusting my greedy cock in and out of his hole.

"FUCKING holy shit man got your damned cock up my ass Chandler!" Ethan panted wildly, and I thought for sure he was going to kick my ass right then and there. "Stretching my ass walls, GAAWWWD..."

"S-sorry man, it seems like my cock has a mind all its own," I grunted, squeezed Ethan's feet tighter yet and drove myself DEEP, DEEP, DEEP inside him.

"ARRRHHH, s-sorry nothing good buddy, that feels amazing, I gotta admit it, SHIIITTT, fucking my hole while you're working and sucking my feet," Ethan garbled crazily. "Never thought it in a million years... what a combo, fucking value meal this is... ARRRHHH yeah..."

That said, Ethan grabbed his cock and began stroking it. He was hard and stacked in no time...

I fucked him harder yet, holding and squeezing and massaging his feet at the same time, the scent of muskiness all over them seeming to drive me on all the more as I fucked and plowed his hole...

"YUHHH... I got me the best fucking roommate at this damned college," Ethan panted and then... "AWWWHHH FUCK man Chandler, I don't believe this shit, but I'm about to shoot my wad from you fucking me and servicing my damned stinky feet... YEAAAHHH fucking A good buddy..."

With that, Ethan stroked his cock harder as my erection slammed in and out of him...

He shot his load like crazy, soaking his upper torso with his mess...

... and then it was my turn buds...

As I again sucked Ethan's toes and as the future NFLer shot the last of his load, I shot my load, cumming inside Ethan's hole.

"MMMHHH..." was the sound I made with my mouth filled with Ethan's toes as I came like gangbusters inside the guy...

"UUUHHH fucking Chandler man, now you really are breeding my shit chute," Ethan grunted, stroking his cock harder yet, getting his balls to give up even more of their thick creamy juices.

When I was done cumming my cock slid slowly out of Ethan's anal canal and I let his toes slip out of my mouth.

We both collapsed onto the floor in front of Ethan's bed, both of us laughing crazily...

"HOOO man, next time you fuck me and worship my feet at the same time I'm gonna be wearing a pair of my silk dress socks... really make sure they stink for you, I'm sure that'll make you fuck me even harder good buddy," Ethan panted and we both laughed harder yet.

The End

Benny's Addiction

"Okay, I admit it, I have an addiction," Benny said to his therapist. Dr. Rack. "It's not a drug or an alcohol addiction... or even a food addiction... it's an addiction to having my cock sucked and my cum swallowed by faggots. I always thought, even as a dude who's married to a woman and who has two teenaged sons that it was no big deal, you know Doc?"

"So, what you're saying Benny, is that you're gay?" Dr. Rack asked his muscular construction worker dark eyed and bearded patient.

"NAH, NAW, nothin' prissy or sissy like that Doc," Benny went on. "I never wanted a relationship with another dude. When it came down to it I wanted what any other normal dude would want, you know, a wife, couple of kids, nice house, maybe a dog... and I got all that, you know?"

As Benny spoke Dr. Rack took notes on his yellow legal pad.

"But as far back as I can remember, even as far back as when I was in high school, oh man, there was just something about having a faggot please me by sucking my cock and scoffing down my cum, even making the fag drink my piss, you know?" Benny went on. "I love dominating faggots. It really puts them in their place you know? Did it for years, even up till now in my mid-thirties Doc. No harm no fouls, just nice macho relief... but then, holy fuck Doc, to have the tables turned on me... GAWD, it was awful, and totally humiliating."

"And just how exactly were the tables turned on you?" Dr. Rack asked the jeans, stained tee shirt and gigantic work booted construction worker.

"Okay Doc, I'm just gonna say it okay?" Benny asked.

"That really is the best way Benny," Dr. Rack replied.

"I was raped by two gay men, AND it was the first time I was even fucked," Benny said, practically choking on his words.

"And how did you feel about that?" Dr. Rack asked.

"How do you think I felt?" Benny asked in reply. "Like I told you, humiliated, but betrayed as well, and totally violated. They fucking turned the tables on me! Turned the goddamned tables on me, JEEZ!"

The doctor nodded and continued writing...

"You see Doc, like I said, for years I've used faggots for quick blowjobs because most women, including my ever loving wife, *won't suck cock*," Benny went on. "But I always refused to suck in return."

"I see," said Dr. Rack. "In other words only gay men suck cock, not straight men."

"Exactly Doc, Ex-fucking-actly," Benny replied and crossed one booted foot over his knee. "So like I said these two faggots in particular, THEY fucking turned the tables on me."

"So you said," Dr. Rack said.

"I had met them in a sleazy fag bar called The Local and we set up a time for me to meet them at their place on a Saturday," Benny said. "My wife knows how I work Saturday's once in a while to earn some extra bucks so setting it up was easy. I was in their bed, laying between them totally fucking naked and in all my muscular glory, and oh man Doc, they were taking turns sucking me, even licking and tongue bathing my big balls. Fuck, I never suspected anything! I never thought for a second what they had in mind.'

Benny paused to take a breath and watched from across the expanse of his chair and the doctor facing him in his chair for any reactions from the man he called his shrink. When he saw none he continued.

"So anyway, they treated me real well those two faggots," Benny said. "I even unloaded two gutsy loads of ball juice on them, and man, they swallowed it down like it was the nectar of the gods. The second time I came one of them sucked my big balls while the other one sucked down my juices. It felt like I had died and gone to cum heaven Doc. I shot so much it was AMAZING…"

"Certainly sounds like it," the doctor said.

"After I was done unloading my second load, the blond dude, a guy named Alex, said it was my turn, that they now wanted me to suck them off," Benny went on, the tone of his voice now sounding both angry and sad. "I quickly told them that I was real thankful for the way they had gotten me off, twice at that, but I went on to tell them that I really was a straight dude and that I did not UNDER ANY CIRCUMSTANCES suck cock! They fucking grinned at each other over me as I lay there and suddenly the more muscular of the two, the brown haired dopey looking one whose name was Ronald pounced on my chest, pinning both my arms down at my sides… AND fuck, he started rubbing his cock all over my face. He pressed it against my lips, smeared his damned pre cum all over my cheeks and told me over and over again how I WAS going to suck cock AND scoff down their cum as well, and as Ronald was doing this Alex was again sucking *my* damned cock. I didn't know if he was fixing to siphon another load from me or if he just wanted to drink my piss, because that's what it felt like. And like most dudes out there, after I've shot a load or two I REALLY need to piss big time!"

"Did you make him drink your urine?" Dr. Rack asked his patient.

"NAH, I never got the chance to do that," Benny went on, sounding miserable now. "Because when I tried to push Ronald off my chest Alex took my cock out of his mouth, grabbed me by the balls and started twisting them real hard. I screamed in an agony I had never known before and Ronald told me to open my mouth wider, as he was again pressing the tip of his erect schlong against my trembling lips."

"Did you open your mouth wider?" Dr. Rack asked.

"I tried not to, I really tried not to," Benny replied. "But the fucking guy kept twisting and yanking harder and harder on my poor balls. It actually felt as if he was going to rip them right off me. AND… to tell it plainly Doc, I felt so fucking ashamed of myself when I felt that damned pre cumming cock on my lips."

"Ashamed how?" Dr. Rack asked, not looking up as he continued writing on his legal pad.

"Well, like I said, I'm a straight dude," Benny said. "It's one thing to have my cock sucked by faggots, but straight guys DO NOT suck cock."

"Yes, so you've stated this," Dr. Rack said softly.

"I cursed at them, threatened them, but the threat of losing my gonads was worse Doc, far fucking worse, so in the end I did as they said," Benny went on. "Ronald wedged himself a bit off my upper body and ordered me to hold my damned arms up and over my head… while they both quickly went to work tying my wrists and arms to the bed board.'

"My goodness, they went so far as to restrain you?" Dr. Rack asked.

"They sure as all fuck did Doc," Benny said. "Fuck, but I was so scared you know? At that point I was begging them to let me go. But that did no good of course. Once I was tied good and tight they said that I needed to be punished for using gay men to satisfy my lustful addiction."

"So you had told them how you considered yourself to be addicted to having gay men suck you off?" Dr. Rack asked.

"Yeah, yeah, I figured they would see it as a compliment, you know?" Benny continued. "But they didn't see it that way Doc. They felt it was wrong for me, a straight married dude to use gay guys to suck me off and not reciprocate. They felt it was totally wrong."

"Did you respond to them where any of that was concerned?" Dr. Rack asked Benny.

"Sure as fuck, I told them to lighten up, to untie me, that it was no big deal, you know?" Benny plowed on, sounding now as if he were pleading his case. "I even suggested, seeing as they were both gay, that they could just suck each other off, how they really didn't need me anymore at that point... but they wouldn't have that either. They told me that it was time that I learned to be a cock sucker. And with that the guy named Ronald went first. He straddled my chest again and aimed his big schlong of a cock toward my mouth. Once more I tried to resist by clamping my mouth shut... but then... oh fuck, fuck being the keyword here, I felt that other guy, Alex, slither two of his fingers into my asshole.

I yelped in pain and anger at the suddenness of it, began to say something like "what the fuck" and as I was speaking Ronald the muscle head filled my mouth with his damned tube steak. My eyes opened wide in total shock as the fucking guy began thrusting his hugeness back and forth in my craw. I could not believe it Doc, I was sucking cock. Ronald told me that if he felt my teeth, even for a second, that he would make short work of me. And let's face it Doc, I really wasn't in any position to argue so I just fucking did as I was being told to do, DAMN, I sucked cock... oh my God Doc, *I sucked cock...*"

"During the time you were forced to perform oral sex on the two men, did you at any given moment find yourself growing aroused Benny?" Dr. Rack asked. "Perhaps even on a subconscious level?"

"That's the *real* shame of it Doc," Benny said. "As I was being made to chow down on Ronald's cock and as Alex was finger fucking my shit chute, getting me ready and primed for an all-out butt fuck-fest, *I did* find myself somehow getting all turned on. It was the craziest thing at that. I mean, I had just shot two loads, two whoppers of loads to be exact... so I really wasn't fully hard in the cock, but my cock was semi hard... and it was tingling too..."

"I see," said Dr. Rack and continued writing on his legal pad.

"After I had been forced to suck Ronald's cock up to a fucking huge erection Alex took his turn fucking my mouth and Ronald diddled and prodded my asshole with his fingers..." Benny said. "Overall they first made me swallow their loads when they shot them the first time... then, after a good fifteen minutes they went to work fucking my poor asshole, my poor up until then virgin asshole Doc..."

"They kept you bound to the bed board as they performed anal sex on you?" Dr. Rack asked, with seeming no emotion behind his words whatsoever.

"Yeah, they did, and to add insult to injury they folded me back on that bed, so that my legs were up in the air as they fucked me six ways from Sunday," Benny said. "I tell you Doc, I felt like a cheap whore on a Saturday night as they fucked me and fucked me. It felt like it would go on forever. They were relentless, taking turns fucking the tar out of me. AND THEN, after they had cum again, this time in my hole, both of them filling me back there with their manly juices, they each popped a goddamned Viagra and went to work fucking me all over again. GOD, by the time they were done my asshole felt like it was minced meat."

"My goodness, it sounds like they really put you through a rather harrowing time," Dr. Rack said.

"That's putting it mildly Doc," Benny said sarcastically. "Harrowing and then some I would call it… I cursed and swore at them, told them how *I* planned to make *short work of them* once I was untied… but they knew I was just blowing smoke. They had bested me Doc. They knew it. They knew they had conquered the straight macho construction worker dude…"

"I see, and that made you feel how?" Dr. Rack asked.

"Humiliated, disgraced, demeaned," Benny said.

"But somehow aroused as well, yes?" Dr. Rack asked.

Benny looked across at the doctor, squinted his eyes for a moment and said, "Jeez Doc, you know me better than I do."

"Not really Benny, I simply know human nature," Dr. Rack replied. "Now tell me, if you would, what did you do after they stopped fucking you and untied you from the bed board?"

"You really need me to tell you that Doc?" Benny asked.

"I think you really need to hear yourself say it Benny," Dr. Rack said.

Benny licked his lips, took a deep breath and said, "Okay Doc, if you say so, I'll tell you. Once they had me untied I grabbed my cock, my hard cock, and started jacking myself off. The pain in my asshole from having been fucked the way they had fucked me seemed to have turned me on like never before in my life... so you see Doc, I used to be addicted to having faggots suck me off, but now, NOW, I'm addicted to having faggots fuck the tar out of me... and then jacking myself off..."

"I see, and how many times have you returned to these two men to have them, as you say, fuck the tar out of you Benny?" Dr. Rack asked.

Benny took another deep breath and said, "Fuck Doc, I've lost count how many times I've gone back to them... to have them fuck the tar out of me..."

As Benny looked at his therapist he saw the doctor look at his crotch. The erection Benny was sporting in his jeans was beyond evident...

"Any further questions Doc?" Benny asked and he noticed the erection that the doctor had in his suit trousers.

"How horny are you at this moment Benny? And how badly do you want that asshole of yours fucked... at this moment?"

The two men looked at each other from across where they were seated across each other, and they smiled devilishly...

Car Ride

Author: Ron Bossman
and added onto by: Christopher Trevor

I was chatting online with Vinny for a while before we finally decided to meet. Since we were both married guys the only available time was early morning when we usually went to the gym. So, on one dark morning at around five AM we met at a coffee shop that was on the highway. I arrived there a bit early. I was wearing exactly what Vinny had told me to wear. He had made me order a pair of gym pants online. They snapped up the side on both sides, allowing them to come off easily and in a hurry. They were also really tight and showed off my religion, as it's been called. I sat in my car in the parking lot of the coffee shop, waiting for Vinny.

A short while later he pulled up beside me. He drove a truck. Vinny worked in construction so early morning was his normal time to go to work. I got out of my car, climbed into the passenger seat of Vinny's truck, said hello to him as he said the same to me, and we took off. I wasn't even sure where he was headed. This was our first meeting and I have to say the guy was fucking hot. Vinny was a good bit shorter than me, but really built, built like a brick shit house, as it's been called. He was Italian and about my age. We had spent many hours online chatting about the things that turned us on so we didn't waste any time getting down to business.

We were heading north up the highway. It was still real dark outside. Vinny told me to take my jacket off and then my tee shirt. I have to say, given my age, I am still in really good shape. The guy was admiring my chest as he drove along. His hand reached over and pinched one of my nipples real hard, getting a few good grunts and groans out of me. I was still wearing the breakaway sweat pants and my underwear and socks and sneakers. Next, Vinny told me to toss my stuff in the back seat and to get the gym bag out from back there. I did as he said and placed the gym bag in front of me. Vinny pulled over.

He opened the bag and pulled out a pair of handcuffs. He ordered me to sit forward in the seat and I did as I was told. Vinny cuffed my hands behind my back. The sound of the handcuffs locking around my wrists was maddening yet totally arousing for me at the same time, as there was an evil grin on Vinny's face. I then sat back with my hands now cuffed behind me. The guy then went for my breakaway gym pants. He ripped them off me, tossed them in the back of the truck and then got my sneakers and socks off me as well, tossing them in the back of the truck as well. I was now sitting there in just my underpants. Vinny took off up the highway. As he drove he kept reaching over and pinching and even twisting my nips, getting me all hard and steamed up in my underpants. And it wasn't long before he pulled over again.

This time he took out a box cutter. My eyes opened wide in fear as I watched as he proceeded to cut my underpants off me, leaving me now totally naked. I was beyond rock hard at that point and I saw from the lamppost that we were parked under that Vinny had a ton of sex toys in his bag. He pulled out a leather slave collar and put it on me, fastening it around my neck, and then a parachute ball stretcher, which he attached to my big hairy balls with a chain leading from it. Without a word he got back in the driver's seat and took off.

Vinny was enjoying watching my situation, me hard and dripping pre cum with a slave collar on and my balls being stretched.

He would pull on my chain as he drove along, which only made matters worse. In other words every time he pulled the chain on the ball stretcher it made me harder and pre cum all the more. And it wasn't too long before he pulled over again. This time the guy took out a pair of tit clamps. Before snapping them onto my nips he gave my nubs a few sucks, slurps and chews, really making them hard and erect, making me grunt and groan like a madman at that point. Vinny then took his sweet time snapping the tit clamps onto my erect and hard nips. He enjoyed seeing the expressions on my face with each new toy he added. Then, he attached the ball stretcher chain to my slave collar, making sure that the chain was nice and tight so that I had to lean over in my seat. Fuck, my balls stretched almost to my mouth.

Vinny loved this. It got him really hard, as I was able to see the bulge in his jeans. He then pulled off the road and started driving through some back roads. After a while he found this dark side road and pulled over. He pulled out his massive Italian sausage sized cock and ordered me to start sucking. I struggled but managed to get down to his cock and I started sucking. It was awesome, fucking amazing actually. He had a huge cock with a big mushroom shaped head. It didn't take Vinny long to getting real close, but he didn't want to cum yet. He was having too much fun with me.

He pulled me off him, I got myself situated back in my seat and we took off again.

We were now traveling down some quiet back roads. Vinny pulled over and told me to climb into the back seat. I somehow managed to get myself back there, seeing as it was tough, being handcuffed and all. But he enjoyed my efforts I must say. Vinny wanted my head on the seat and my ass in the air. I did as I was instructed and once in position he again attached my ball chain to my slave collar. This caused my balls to pull under me and made my cock SO hard.

Vinny got some lube out of his bag and started fingering my hole. Then he worked a small butt-plug into my ass. He teased me by saying that that should keep me for a bit. Then, he got back in the driver's seat and took off yet again. I couldn't see where he was going at this point. Every now and then he would glance back at me, and then he pulled over again. We were deep in the woods and on some quiet road. Vinny came to the back seat and pulled out his cock. He whipped the butt-plug out of my ass and it was quickly replaced by his cock. Damn, that man was HUGE. He fucked me real well, really stretching my ass walls. When he was done, after he had shot a huge whopper of a load into my guts and jacked me off as well he got me back in the front seat. I was still handcuffed and wearing my slave collar, tit clamps and ball stretcher. After a while he took those items off me and made me stay naked until we got back to the coffee shop parking lot. This was nerve-racking, as it was starting to get light out. I was worried that drivers of other trucks or cars would see me naked as the day I was born in Vinny's truck.

After a significant amount of whining on my part Vinny allowed me to put my jacket back on. We pulled up next to my car. I quickly put my pants back on minus my shredded underwear. We said good-bye and I wondered what our next ride would be like.

The End?

About the Author

     Christopher Trevor was born in July 1963 and grew up in New York City. As soon as he was old enough to know how he began writing fiction and has been writing gay erotic/fetish stories for the past ten to twelve years at this point. He became an avid reader as well from the time he knew how and reads everything from fiction, to non-fiction to biographies of interesting and unusual people, people who have made a difference or who have paved the way for others. Christopher attributes his writing artistic inspiration to artists such as Etienne, Tom of Finland, Tagame, The Hun, and most notably Joe T, who Christopher has had the pleasure of speaking with and even meeting over the last few years. Christopher states, "Joe T encouraged me to write about my fetish because I was embarrassed about it at the time. Joe T said that when we are embarrassed about some- thing that makes it even more enticing somehow." Christopher totally agreed and never stopped writing in this genre. Erotic writers who inspired Christopher Trevor were: Tom Shaw (author of "That Day at the Quarry), C.S. White (author of Big Sur), Larry Townsend (author of countless erotic novels), and Mason Powell (author of the classic story "The Brig.")

Christopher discovered that not only did he enjoy writing erotic tales but that after his first bondage experience he had a genuine flair for it. Writing to erotic oriented magazines about his first bondage experience truly opened the floodgates for Christopher where this style of writing is concerned. Christopher thanks the handsome and muscular "Greg" for that experience way back in time. Christopher took "Creative Writing" courses every semes- ter during his high school years and while other friends of his stopped writ- ing what they loved to write about as time went on Christopher never let a day go by when he didn't write something... "I feel that if I don't write every day I will die," Christopher has said many times over.

Foot fetish stories and all things related; spanking fetish, erotic shaving, muscle bondage, tickle torture, and hardcore stories are just a few of the areas of gay eroticism that Christopher enjoys writing about and inspiring in others as well. As one internet buddy said to Christopher where the black socks fetish is concerned, "Until I started talking with you I never gave a thought to my socks when I got dressed for work in the morning. Now when I pull my dress socks on every morning I get a chill up my spine."

Christopher is proud of the erotic effect he has on people...